The Secret Warrior

NEST LUMSDEN

Table of Contents

Phoebe, who gave me inspiration.

Debbie, who gave me much needed support.

ABOUT THE AUTHOR

Born in Germany, the daughter of a British army officer; Nest settled in rural Lincolnshire, where she enjoys working on her allotment and watching birds. Apart from writing, her interests include playing the piano and drawing. Sipping a pint in a pub is also a favourite pastime.

CHAPTER ONE

The gamekeeper knew where the nest was. He had seen the harriers flying over the heather, the female carrying plant stems and grass to layer the nest hidden on the ground. Bates watched her effortless, sailing flight, wings held in a slight "V", hunting over the open terrain, then swooping down on voles and small birds. He held the rifle close to his body, scanning the heather and the wood beyond, wondering if he was being watched. There didn't seem to be anyone around, although he knew all the tricks which those "birders" got up to; they had caught him before. Then there was that boy. He clenched his fist as he thought about him. What a pest he was, always hanging around, trespassing, following him and spying. The little creep! Roger Bates, a lean, athletic-looking man in his early fifties, had one aim that morning: to kill a pair of hen harriers and destroy their nest quickly and efficiently. His employer should be grateful to him. After all, the revenue which the annual grouse shoot brought in every year was largely because of his efforts. Besides, no one had specifically told him not to kill birds of prey. Of course, it was illegal, but he had escaped prosecution. Then Ethan Elliot moved to the area. That boy was more like a shadow than a human being, appearing out of nowhere. Young and agile, always one step ahead of him. Bates was feeling the effects of working outside, whatever the weather. It was becoming harder to leave his warm bed in the morning, and his back was often stiff and painful. Sometimes, he experienced stabbing pains down his left leg, which his doctor told him was sciatica. Whatever it was, it was bloody painful. That's all he knew.

Now, someone was there, just on the edge of the moor, by the tree line. Bates searched the area with his binoculars. No one, but he was sure...well, he couldn't stand here all day; he had a job to do. Bates walked on slowly, looking for the harriers. It was drizzling, so he hid the binoculars under his coat and put the hood over his head. The female was flying again. He was close enough to shoot her. He angled his rifle...crack! His head spun. What was happening to him? What was going on? His head hurt, and there was blood. Someone had attacked him... As he hit the ground, Bates saw a blurred vision of someone running away in a green waxed jacket. He would remember that.

CHAPTER TWO

Ethan stood in front of his scrupulously clean washbasin and washed his hands. His mother had taught him how to do this properly. Taking two squeezes of liquid soap and a little water, he rubbed the back of his hands, repeating this action with the palms, followed by the thumbs and wrists. Satisfied his hands were clean, he rinsed and carefully dried them on a soft blue towel, one of many, which he stored in a cabinet next to the sink. Ethan was a young man in his twenties, not tall, like many of his contemporaries, but with a strong, stocky physique. He kept his wiry, sandy-coloured hair short. His face was pleasant, some would say handsome, and clear blue eyes always ready to catch the slightest movement, or change in the weather. He had finely tuned this ability over years of spending his free time in the woods and fields near his home and hours wandering over his beloved moors. He lived with his parents, Susan and Peter and his sister, Mattie, on their farm near the Forest of Bowland in Lancashire, an area of farming and moorland, the latter being used for the annual red grouse shoot.

He dressed quickly, taking his clothes from the neatly folded pile on a high-backed chair, brushed his hair and teeth, then stood for a few minutes, looking out of the window. He could see the grazing sheep on the hills, and fields surrounded by dry-stone walls, so typical of the area. Although he had not taken to farming, Ethan loved to help with the maintenance and repairing of the walls, continuing the old traditions. His gaze turned to the patchwork of small in-bye fields further away, surrounded by hedgerows, leading down to the valleys and woodland and the larger walled areas. These contained a mixture of flock-hill breeding ewes and suckler beef herds, the land not being suited to dairy farming, because of the climate, topography and the remoteness of much of the area. His parents had not been born into farming. Peter had taken an enormous gamble when he bought Moor Farm, but he had managed, through hard work and sheer determination, to make it work. Ethan had watched him struggle, especially in the early days and his father's disappointment with his son's unwillingness to take more interest in the farm.

Ethan's thoughts turned to the moors. He loved the remoteness, the colours of the heather and all the secret places where he liked to walk. It was a man-made environment, specifically managed for the shooting and the heather burning in October, thus encouraging fresh growth from mid-August until the middle of December. He walked on the moors most days unless his father needed his help urgently, but his major concern was always out there, with the welfare and protection of the birds of prey which bred amongst the heather or lived in the area. Ethan was well aware of their continued persecution, the poisoning and shooting, eggs that were crushed, nests destroyed by the gamekeepers... and of one man in particular, Roger Bates, Head Gamekeeper on the estate.

Ethan went downstairs into the kitchen where breakfast was being cooked by Susan on an old, blackened range which had been part of the kitchen for about two hundred years. Much of the interior had been modernised, but the beams, flooring and windows had survived. The rest comprised modern units, with space for a washing machine, dishwasher and fridge/freezer. Susan had insisted on keeping the range as it still cooked superbly.

She was a petite, pretty woman in her mid-fifties, still keeping her long hair in a plait during the day and "setting it free" in the evening or when she went out. It was wonderful hair: thick, soft auburn tresses and not a single grey strand. She had not wanted to move from their well-ordered and comfortable life in Derbyshire to move to a hill farm in Lancashire, something that was totally alien to her. She still could not understand Peter's decision to move. To her, it was bordering on insanity, sinking all their savings and selling their lovely house, as well as using his redundancy money to buy the farm. She had argued and argued with him, hoping he would drop his ridiculous dream, see sense and be content with the life he had, but it was useless. When considering her own options, she had agreed with his plans, but only if he accepted her conditions. If Peter's enterprise failed, he would be on his own. She would not be responsible for the financial consequences and would leave him. Then, he would have to provide a decent house for her and the children if they lived with her. Her second condition was that her role was to keep the house as she had always done and not help on the farm unless she wanted to. That was the deal; take it, or he would have to move on his own.

Peter agreed. What choice did he have? He had to realise an alarming and for him, a sad truth. Susan didn't love him and perhaps never had. He had assumed that she wanted what he did and would fall in with his plans without question. Her demands were completely unexpected. Facing him in their living room, she had remained strong and resolute, leaving him without a choice. If they put all their money into this venture, he must make it work. But, after the move, Peter had to accept that Ethan had little interest in the farm, and he had worked himself into a state of near exhaustion, building up his herd and a flock of sheep. Still, Mattie loved the farm, and when not at school or doing homework, she worked with him, and slowly they made progress. He also had help from a local farmer, Jack Field, who gave Peter help and guidance. Jack was a widower and a lonely man who soon became part of the family. Despite initial setbacks, Peter was making the farm work.

Mattie was fifteen and clearly took after her mother physically. Although her nose was a little long, her mouth a little wide, she had an unusual beauty. Her hair was the same colour as Susan's, but she kept it short and urchin-like. It was her eyes which held people's attention: big and deep green. The overall impression of Mattie was of a strange and other-worldly imp or sprite. She was fiercely loyal to Peter.

One morning Peter and Mattie came in for breakfast, having been working together with the cows. Susan turned around when she heard the door open. 'Just look at the state of your boots. Nevermind, take them off and sit down. I wasn't expecting you for breakfast so early. Food won't take long to cook.'

'That's great,' replied Peter, pulling off his boots and leaving them outside the kitchen door. 'A tough morning, cutting silage for the herd, and the winter fodder is running out fast. I'm worried about some cows. I'll ask Jack to look at them before I call the vet. Need to make sure it's not Bovine Virus Diarrhoea.'

'Yes, Peter,' interrupted Susan, 'I'm sure we don't want to talk about that at breakfast. Just get the vet in; that's best. More expense, I suppose. Still, just one of the many pitfalls of having cattle.'

They ate breakfast in silence, each family member thinking about their day ahead. Peter would be busy on the farm; the health of his cows was always a worry for him. Early March and getting ready to put them out to pasture, although he would still have to provide them with supplementary feeding. They were carefully divided into groups according to their body condition, and he prayed they were all free from infection. If they had a viral disease, it could spread between the animals or from mother to calf during pregnancy, causing embryonic deaths, abortions and reduced fertility. The last thing he wanted was barren cows and the financial loss this would cause.

Mattie had fallen behind with her homework and the revision for her exams. She knew her father was worried, needing her help with the cows, but in the coming week he would have to manage on his own. Mike, the vet, could treat the herd if needed, but she knew they were well because of her uncanny knack of knowing precisely about the health of the herd and the flocks of sheep. In fact, valuable animals had been saved in the past because of her timely observations. Mattie knew Peter was struggling to keep the farm going, and he worried constantly. She didn't blame her mother, who hadn't wanted the move and had made her position clear. She was a wonderful mother, always there if Mattie needed her, especially with end-of-year exams looming.

Susan had her own secrets, something that had taken her quite by surprise. Her life, which mainly consisted of looking after the house, doing shopping and helping Mattie with her schoolwork, was more interesting by meeting Jack Field. At first, she had taken little notice of him. Just another slightly grizzled farmer who often came to the farm to help Peter. She knew Jack's advice was critical to Peter's survival. Then, one day, when the children were out, and Peter had just driven off to get supplies, Jack came around. He knew she was on her own and seemed in no hurry to leave. So, she made tea, and they talked. Susan found him good company, telling her jokes and interesting stories about his life. He attracted her partly because he was so different from Peter. He wasn't tall like him but was strong and kept himself fit through years of constant hard physical work. A little thin on top, but that didn't matter. His deep brown eyes looked at her keenly, and the attraction became mutual. After that, Susan invited him around whenever she was on her own. Sometimes, she walked to his farm. To his surprise, she even took an interest in his sheep, dotted about on the hillside, or wondering what bird it was that sang so loudly from a branch overhead. Feeling guilty, she even showed some interest in Peter's work, which pleased him, although he couldn't understand why. Jack had lived on his own for six years. His relationship with Susan was as rewarding and exciting as it was for her, outweighing his sense of guilt. No one would know if they were careful.

Then the day came when Susan moved out of the bedroom she shared with Peter, moving into the spare room, which doubled up as the study. Peter would have to keep his farm records and accounts somewhere else; she needed her own space, privacy and personal things around her. Of course, it hurt Peter, telling Susan that 'sleeping in another room was tantamount to living separately. The next thing would be her moving out altogether. Is that what she wanted?' Susan reminded him of the fact there was no intimacy between them anymore and that she needed her own space. The arrangement was the way it would have to be. Her favourite old bear sat on a chair by her bed. Books and plants filled the shelves, small, cosy and always warm. Peter wouldn't wake her with his early morning starts either.

Ethan considered himself something of a warrior. He wouldn't be joining marches or holding up traffic on the motorway. His concerns were local. At school, he was called "the snail" because of a time when, after a period of heavy rain, he had rescued as many snails as possible from the paths adjoining the playground to stop them from being crushed by boys whom he knew had no souls. He ignored their taunts and, towards the end of this final year, he left school, refusing to go back. Susan supported his decision, telling the authorities that Ethan was being bullied and because he only had a few months to go, she wouldn't be sending him back. He could always go to college to take exams if he wanted to.

Ethan put on his green camouflage jacket and trousers, stuffed a balaclava into his pocket and put a day's supply of food, tea and water into his rucksack. He strung his binoculars around his neck and went downstairs. Peter was talking to the vet, and Susan was washing up. Ethan told her he was going and was likely to be away for most of the day. Susan worried about Ethan. He walked on the moors all the time and she knew about Bates, who sounded a very nasty piece of work. Ethan had told her he had to protect the birds which nested there. Bates often saw him but would never catch him. Besides, there were other concerned bird lovers with whom he shared information. He had his phone with him and promised to call her if he was in trouble. Susan stood at the door, watching him go. She couldn't stop him but was proud of him too. Peter was nowhere to be seen, probably in the cowshed. She saw Mike and waved to him as he drove away before retreating into the house. Making herself a coffee, she sat for a while, planning her next trip to Jack's farm.

CHAPTER THREE

Leona sat with eyes closed, meditating, something she did every morning, finding this practice calming and a useful aid before her first client arrived. She was a clairvoyant with thirty year's experience, precise and practised in her work, which she took seriously. The gift of premonition often caused her anxiety, as she saw things that she kept to herself, especially when it concerned death, illness or other tragic events. It all depended on the client, on that person's strength and ability to handle bad news, and she sensed that clearly. They had a choice of cards, tarot, rune stones and even tea leaf readings, an old but often reliable means of information. The clients were, inevitably, mostly women seeking help when traditional methods had failed or when personal support from partners or friends was missing from their lives. Visitors were not confined to the local area because Leona was a well-known and respected clairvoyant, and people travelled to see her from all over the country. In the past, she had travelled extensively but didn't do that anymore, preferring to stay at home, letting people come to her strictly by appointment only. Leona's world was indeed a strange one; half received messages and voices, sometimes disjointed or whispered. So many people are in need of reassurance, clarification or re-connection with their lives.

Leona was not looking forward to her first client, Mavis Wilson, a deeply troubled young woman desperate for a baby with a history of miscarriages. When she arrived, Leona showed her into the small dining room reserved for her readings. Everything here conferred peace and comfort with soft cushions, candles, sweet-smelling incense and, of course, copious amounts of tea and homemade biscuits.

Mavis sat at the table, with Leona opposite, who smiled and said, 'How have you been since our last meeting, Mavis?'

Mavis sighed, close to tears. 'I feel a little better. It certainly helps to come to see you. It's awful at home; it really is. John doesn't understand how I feel, and he's told me not to come and see you again. Anyway, he can say what he likes. He can't stop me, although I wait until he's gone to work. The consultant tells me not to worry and that the baby is doing fine, but I just can't help it. I want this baby so much.'

'Well,' replied Leona, 'I'm sure he's right, Mavis, and worrying all the time won't help, now will it? You must learn to relax and calm down; I'm not sure that another reading will help. Perhaps you should go home now? Come back in a few weeks when the situation is clearer.'

Mavis looked alarmed. 'Oh please, Leona, I must have a reading. I need to know to be sure. I can't go home yet; I really can't. Just one reading. Please!'

Leona felt slightly irritated. If the reading didn't go the way Mavis wanted, it would cause her more grief, and she would have to deal with her distress. She wouldn't lie to her either but could try to be non-committal, saying the reading was not clear, suggesting again that she come back another time. Oh well, a reading it was then.

'Very well, Mavis. How about a tea leaf reading this time? It's easy and quick and should give me something to work with. Give me your cup carefully.'

Mavis's face brightened. She handed over her cup, trying to read Leona's face. Leona drained the cup, closed her eyes for a few seconds and looked at the jumble of leaves. There was no doubt she could see the baby but not the face. The baby would be stillborn. How was she going to tell Mavis this news?

Mavis leaned across the table. 'Is it good news? Please tell me, Leona. I want to know either way. I must know.'

'I'm not sure, Mavis, the reading's blurred. It happens sometimes with the leaves. Come and see me in a few weeks so that I can make an accurate reading.'

'You're lying to me. I know you are. My baby's going to die, and you don't want to tell me.' Mavis was crying uncontrollably now. Grabbing her coat and bag, she ran towards the door. Leona followed her. 'Listen to me, Mavis. You will have a healthy baby. Just not...'

Leona cleared the crockery and prepared herself for the next client. Mavis's session had shaken her. She did her best to help people by interpreting the signs, but she was not responsible for what she read there. Dawn would be here soon, a gentle, thoughtful woman who had lost her husband recently. Just a little reassurance to help with the grieving process, and she would provide that. Leona never charged a fee for this service.

'Come in, Dawn, so good to see you. How are you feeling today? We'll just sit quietly like last time.' Leona could see the shadowy outline of Dawn's husband, Michael, standing by the side of his wife. Leona smiled and said, 'Michael's here and standing by you. You may feel his presence. He sends his love and tells you he is fine. You must not worry about him. Look after the children and know that you are never alone.'

Dawn was glad she had come and very grateful to this remarkable woman. She would continue to need her services for a while yet, but, in time, she would fully accept her husband's death and move on. For now, she was happy just sitting here with Leona in this cosy room, sipping tea and savouring the comfort it had brought her.

When Dawn had gone, Leona rang the last client of the day and rearranged the appointment. She was exhausted, wanting to be on her own for the rest of the day and recover.

An hour later, Mavis's husband, John, was banging on her door. It wasn't the first time Leona had faced an angry husband. It might be part of her job, but it certainly shouldn't be. What was the difference between a doctor telling someone the truth and her doing so? To her knowledge, she had never told a client anything which failed to materialise, but she sometimes got the blame for it. Should she open the door and try to explain or ring the police? Leona secured the door chain first.

'What the hell did you think you were doing, telling my wife the baby would die? The doctors don't think there's anything wrong! There's a healthy baby in there, you stupid bitch! Mavis is in the right state, and it's your fault. She won't stop crying, and I don't know what to do.' John Wilson was a big, overweight man, quick to lose his temper. Leona had to get rid of him. She said, as calmly as she could, 'I'm sorry about Mavis, but I didn't force her to come and see me. What she needs now is your support. You need to calm down and give her whatever comfort you can. See the consultant again and get another opinion. Of course, it will be best if Mavis doesn't come to me for a while. Now, I want you to leave my property, or I will call the police.'

John Wilson strode away from the house, and Leona watched him go. It had rained, and she was about to close and lock the door when she saw a woman trying to take shelter under the large chestnut tree at the bottom of the garden. 'Hello, can I help you? Have you come to see me?'

The woman walked a little way up the garden path. The rain was heavy now, and she was shivering with the cold. 'Sorry, I was taking shelter under the tree. I'll make my way home now.'

'Wait,' called Leona, 'come inside for a while and get warm. I have spare clothes you can borrow. I can sense you need help.'

The woman's name was Mona. She lived in one of the older houses a few streets away. This morning, she had gone into the garden and listened to the beautiful, repetitive song of the song thrush, and a robin had dropped near her, eating the meal worms she had placed for it. Six months ago, she had made a terrible mistake and was suffering for it. She left her home and went to live with her ex-husband, in the firm belief that she still loved him, and for the first six months, there had been relative happiness. After all, wasn't that what they both wanted to finish what they had started years ago when they had been so happy before it went wrong? Why had she thought it would be different now? Malcolm was a good man, he had tried hard to make it work. It was no good. The doubts came, not slowly but suddenly, and with it, depression and anxiety. Well, she'd believed in a false dream, convincing herself that friendship was true love, and now, she had to do something about it. They had divorced ages ago, so she had no rights to the house. Malcolm knew something was wrong. Mona was distant, kept to herself, didn't want to spend time with him and slept in the box room. She felt trapped but blamed no one but herself.

Not only that, but she had brought her ten-year-old daughter, Mollie, with her. Somehow, she had to find somewhere decent to live and start again. For the moment, she did what had to be done, but as time went by, she dreaded Malcolm coming home from work and spent the evenings and weekends with Mollie, trying to avoid Malcolm as much as possible. Today, when Mollie was at school, she wandered away from home, not caring where she went. Following a few country paths, she ended up near some woods. She wouldn't go there today because there wasn't time, and it had rained, so she turned back. A young man passed her and said 'hello' and walked on. He seemed to know where he was going, anyway. She watched him go into the darkness of the woods with his rucksack and binoculars; he seemed on a mission. Eventually, Mona sheltered under an enormous tree. Ten minutes later, she was offered a towel, dry clothing and a hot drink.

CHAPTER FOUR

They had admitted Bates to the hospital for initial treatment for his head wound and to make sure nothing more serious had occurred. However, a brain scan revealed nothing worrying, just a slight concussion and some confusion of the events leading up to the attack. He insisted on a visit from the police; he knew the name of his attacker. No, he didn't have actual proof it was Ethan, but that boy had been stalking him for months now. Every day, he was there, sometimes on the edge of the moor but usually well inside it. Apart from anything else, he was guilty of trespass and needed talking to.

'I see, sir,' said P.C. Short, 'We will question this boy as part of our enquiries, but do you have actual proof he attacked you?'

'No, but it was him. Who else could it have been? I know the person who hit me was wearing one of those green, waxed jackets, and that's exactly what he wears. Needs locking away so I can get on with my job.'

P.C. Short wrote a few notes in his notebook and left Bates with an assurance that further enquiries would be made and the gamekeeper informed of the outcome. If he could remember any other details of the attack, he was to inform them immediately.

The next day Bates was discharged with painkillers, which he washed down with a swig of whiskey. Maybe he should have lied to the police, telling them he saw Ethan up close to him just before the attack, but then thought better of that idea. How he hated that boy! Eventually, he would get his own back and make him suffer.

The police car parked in the farmyard where Peter and Jack were working. News of the attack on Bates had made the rounds of the village, and the police were making general enquiries. Their arrival alarmed Peter; he showed them into the house, followed by Jack, who took charge of the situation. 'If this is about the attack on Bates, you've come to the wrong address, officer. Bates is a brute and is disliked by everyone. Anyone of a dozen people could have attacked him. You know, I suppose that he breaks the law regularly; he kills raptors, which are protected by law.' P.C. Short raised his hand and said, 'And you are?'

'Jack Field, a friend of the family. I have a farm a few miles away.'

'Right,' answered the constable, turning to address Peter. 'I would like to have a word with Ethan. I assume you are his father?'

Susan heard the voices and came downstairs with Ethan. 'I'm Susan Elliot, and this is my son, Ethan. What's this all about?'

'I'm making enquiries concerning an assault on Mr Bates, a local gamekeeper, which occurred on February the nineteenth. Whoever it was waited until about four-thirty, just as it was getting dark. Your son, Ethan, was mentioned as a suspect in the attack. Let me clarify: I am not making any arrests. I just want to talk to him.'

'Sure, I'm Ethan, but I had nothing to do with it.'

'Can you remember where you were at the time of the attack? I believe you are a frequent visitor to the moor, where Mr Bates works. Do you own a green waxed jacket?'

'I was checking on bird boxes all that week and some volunteering for the local wildlife trust, including the day you mentioned. I was home well before dark, about two.'

'Ethan has a green jacket,' broke in Susan, 'I'll get it for you, officer.' She came back with four green jackets, all waxed and similar to each other. 'This is Ethan's jacket, but, as you can see, we all have one. In fact, lots of people wear them around here because they're warm and waterproof. You have one too, don't you, Jack?'

Jack smiled. 'Yes, I do. Shall I fetch it?'

P.C. Short frowned. 'Yes, o.k. I get the joke, Mrs Elliot. I have no more questions for the moment, but I would advise you not to go anywhere near Mr Bates, Ethan. He is in an ugly mood at the moment. Don't go onto the moor either, as it will be trespassing. The police do all they can to protect the birds which frequent and nest in the area. We will monitor the situation. I may need to talk to you again, Ethan. Thank you all for your time.'

Peter returned to the yard. Surely Ethan had nothing to do with the attack on that awful man? He just wanted to get on with farming and not be bothered with gamekeepers and police. Wonderful, the way Susan neatly rounded off the interview by producing not one but four green jackets. He would never have thought of doing that. He wished they were closer, like in the early days of their marriage. Maybe it wasn't too late, though. He would make more of an effort, maybe take her out for a meal, make time away from the farm to spend together. Jack was a good friend; maybe he would confide in him and ask for advice.

Jack joined Peter. He said little; he was feeling guilty. Which relationship was more important to him, Peter or Susan? He supposed the affair would run its course, but if Peter discovered the truth in the meantime, it would ruin their friendship. Helping Peter with the farm had not only ended his crushing loneliness but had given his life a new purpose. His expertise and years of farming were something that he could impart to Peter. He felt so useful and valued and wanted to spend more time with this like- minded man and cut down on his visits to see Susan.

Susan watched Jack leave while Peter disappeared into the shed. She felt annoyed; what was Jack playing at? He usually called in before going home, but then, he had been less friendly lately. A hint that things were cooling for him? She put on her walking boots and jacket and left the house. Walking past Jack's farm, she carried on to the village, stopping at the church. Susan was not interested in the names written on the gravestones. Instead, she searched around them, looking for wildflowers in the overgrown meadow grass, like dead souls which had sprung to life. Here, she found red poppies, ox-eyed daisies and yellow rattle. Lichens grew on the stones, some bright yellow, others orange, grey and green. Thankfully, there were no new black polished headstones on which nothing grew. Walking up to the church door, she pushed the latch; it opened. Very peaceful, and no one else to spoil her visit.

Susan had not been to a service for some time. Some of her religious views were certainly unconventional, although she considered herself a Christian. She just didn't want to become too involved. People wanted to know who she was, would she volunteer for the next event? They meant well and acted with the best of intentions, but their over-friendliness had stopped her going again. Then, there was the question of where non-human life fitted into the Church and Christianity. Why was it always about people,while so little was said about animals? Susan sat down, closed her eyes and said a prayer for her family, Jack and all the endangered animals and birds in the world.

Leaving the church, she found a public right of way, taking her over fields and streams, eventually leading to an extensive wood on the right. Should she explore there? She enjoyed walking through trees. No, today the wood didn't seem inviting, so she walked on until she came to the start of the intensive moors, and here she stopped. A pair of buzzards called to each other, circling, eventually disappearing over the wood. They would be safer there, that's for sure, Susan thought. At least the gamekeeper was nowhere in sight; that was one person she did not want to meet.

She turned back, making her way to the local pub, "The Curlew". She often called in here, sitting on her own, away from the bar and the chatter of the farmers or visitors. No one bothered her here. She ordered a pint of the recommended local ale and a sandwich and sat by the window and relaxed. Having time away from the farm helped Susan to focus on her life and those of the people she loved. When Peter had first told her of his plans to buy the farm, she had been incongruous. What a stupid, ill-thought idea that she was being asked to be a part of. She had agreed to it, with certain conditions, which Peter had agreed to. Well, to Susan's surprise, her husband was actually making a success of her venture, and yes, she was happy for him.

Then, Jack came into her life; things became exciting, and she had something to look forward to. As long as no one else knew, the affair would take its course. Susan took each day at a time. No good ever came of thinking too far ahead, especially after this morning. Why hadn't Jack come into the house? Not even popping in to say "goodbye". Was he having second thoughts about their relationship? Feeling guilty, perhaps? Well, despite everything, so was she. So, the alternative for both of them was a loveless marriage for her and a lonely existence for Jack. Did he really want that? Susan's thoughts turned to Ethan and Mattie. She couldn't leave them, so, for the foreseeable future, her place was at the farm. Mattie, to Susan's astonishment, loved farm life; she had already gained so much experience and knowledge and could take over the farm one day. As for Ethan, his future was uncertain. He was heavily involved with his volunteering and helping bird organisations tackle the persecution of raptors. And then, there was Bates.

The pub was getting busy. Susan bought another drink. There was no hurry to get back, was there? She heard a lot of laughing and loud talking coming from the table nearest the bar. A strange-looking man walked in and was soon the hub of much attention. A local countryman and well-respected, Dulap Whottle was an eccentric resident of the area, having lived all his life in the district. No one was sure of his age; sixty, sixty-five, seventy? A thin, wiry, but strong man, he wore his long grey hair tied in a plait down his back; his clothes were colourful, and he always wore an old battered hat sporting a pheasant feather in its brim. Susan was interested. Who was this character? He was certainly well-liked. She moved tables to hear everything that was being said. He never bought his own drinks because people kept Dulap supplied with his favourite beer.

A regular, Pete Davis, asked, 'Nice to see you, Dulap, we haven't seen you recently. Where have you been hiding?'

'Oh, here and there, here and there. Matters to attend to, you know. What's this I've been hearing about that old devil, Bates? Been killing birds again, has he?' Dulap turned and looked at Susan, smiling at her. Why had he done that? Was he implying that he knew something about her or Ethan?

The customers duly informed Dulap of what had occurred on the moor. Someone had bashed Bates, but the police had dropped the case through lack of evidence. Dulap laughed, then finished his pint. Someone duly supplied another, to which he said, 'thanks, mate; serves the bastard right, what's what I say. Many a time I've stopped his games, and he's never known it was me. Not that I'm saying I hit him on the head; plenty of others who take an interest in his activities. The police won't get information out of me.' Dulap walked up to Susan and said, 'Who are you then? Can't say as I've seen you in here before. You make a pleasant addition, though.' The whole pub was now focused on Susan. She felt uncomfortable and didn't want to be the centre of attention. Still, what could she do?

'My name's Susan. I live with my family at Moor Farm. Nice to meet you. Dulap, is it? An unusual name. I like it, though.'

'Thanks,' replied Dulap, 'don't rightly know where the name came from. Good pub this, plenty of pals to drink with. Having a crafty one, away from the family, are we? Don't blame you, Susan;

everyone needs time on their own to unwind and take stock.' Susan was embarrassed; she didn't like being singled out. Was Dulap ridiculing her in front of the whole pub? Now, whenever she came in, she might be recognised and wasn't sure she liked that. Still, she couldn't help liking this man, feeling he would be a useful friend to have around. Besides, he was certainly no friend of the gamekeeper. Finishing her drink, she quickly left the pub. Looking at her watch and realising she had been away about two hours, she made her way back, hoping Jack would not be there. If the relationship were over, she would rather not know yet. That way, there was always the hope she had misunderstood Jack's avoidance of her.

Peter was busy with the twin lambs inside the sheep sheds after the lambing season. Last year's female lambs had to be treated for scabelice, and mothers with young were to be put back on the fells, which ran alongside the pasture land. Then, the twins would join the single lambs. Mattie had been helping Peter. She had marked each ewe with a coloured ear tag, which recorded which tup had served which female. She also took care of the flock records so they could trace the parentage of each individual sheep's family tree come selling time. They gave this year's and last year's ewes pink tags; otherwise, the tags were blue. Mattie also helped to mark each sheep with the farm's unique sign.

'Hello, Peter, how are things going? Many twins this year?' Peter looked up in surprise. Susan had never taken an interest in his work before.

'Oh, yes, about average. I've been really busy with lambing. Couldn't have done it without Mattie's help. Still, the lambs are going out with the ewes, and the mothers won't need feeding, so, apart from watching out for worms, which can kill a lamb, it will be a quieter time for me. Now, the cows need attention. Twelve weeks of calving, then out to pasture, with supplementary feeding, in the uplands. Sorry Susan, too much information, I expect.' Susan smiled. 'No, not really. I can see how busy you are, so I'll leave you to it. Is Mattie home?'

'Yes, she went in about an hour ago.'

Susan found Mattie in the kitchen, doing homework. 'Hello Mum. I wondered where you were. Is everything o.k?'

'Yes, Mattie, I think so. I saw your Dad on the way to the house. It surprised him when I asked him how lambing was going. I do like to see the newborns; so sweet, aren't they? Anyway, he talked a bit about what he was doing with the sheep and the cows. It was quite interesting, really. You really love helping, don't you, Mattie?'

'Yes, I do, Mum. As soon as I can, I shall work on the farm full-time. I'm not even sure about going to college.'

'It might be a good idea to get some farming qualifications, Mattie, just in case your Dad ever had to give the farm up. He's doing well, but it's early days. Farming can be risky at the best of times. Still, I'm so pleased you know what you want. Your father and I will give you all the help and support you need.'

'Thanks, Mum. Can I ask you something personal about you and Dad?'

'Of course, Mattie. Go ahead.'

'Well, I just wanted to know if you still loved Dad. I know you don't share the same room anymore, and you don't seem as close.'

'I don't love your Dad as you want me to; that's true. I'm still very fond of him and we do share this home. I can't help the way I feel, but I'm a lot happier than I was. In a way, it's also given me a fresh start too. I enjoy living in the countryside and going for walks. I even call into the pub sometimes. There are some interesting people living in or near the village, and I enjoy having time to myself. Maybe I could take up a new interest? Ethan could teach me all about his birds. I know I take little interest in the farm, but for now, I'm happy to be here. Does that answer your question?'

'Yes, I suppose it does. I'll finish my homework and see if Dad needs help. See you later.'

After supper, Susan sat in the garden just as it was getting dark. There was a full moon, and it was dazzling. Grey clouds drifted in front of it, like a scene from an old movie. She felt content and safe, a total part of the nature that enclosed her.

CHAPTER FIVE

Leona's mother lost her powers in her mid-fifties, the age Leona was now. It had started with a gradual inability to read the signs correctly, and within one year, she had lost her clientele. Leona expected the same would happen to her. Over many years, she had saved a considerable amount of money to compensate for future loss of earnings. However, she had not lost her powers; in fact, they had developed to such a degree that it was frightening her. Some of her regulars had stopped coming because of the gossip about Mavis, but many more continued to have faith in her. Her reputation was intact; she had more clients than before. Mona had become a good friend who, despite often visiting Leona, had never asked for a reading. Instead, she asked for conventional advice about her problems.

'It's never a good idea to rekindle an old love,' Leona said. 'How long were you apart?'

'Oh, it must have been about ten years. We started meeting up for drinks and meals, and, of course, that was fun. I moved into his house, and within six months, I regretted it. All the problems we had before were still there, of course. Now, I have to leave a second time, and it won't be easy because I have nowhere to move to. I have applied to the council, and it might be possible to get a small house on the recent development nearby.'

'Well, you have a dependent child to look after, so I'm sure that you will get something soon. In the meantime, try to keep busy if you can. You can visit me whenever you like, as long as I'm not working. Just text me, and I'll let you know when I'm free.' Leona stopped talking and rushed into the other room, just in time to reach her armchair before a vision began, which would have left her incapable of standing. She saw figures, a face and then a light so bright she could not see. As it faded, she closed her eyes and groaned.

Mona had followed her. ' Leona, what's the matter? Are you ill?'

'No, I'll be fine; just give me a few minutes, Mona. This keeps happening to me. I don't know why, though I'm not surprised; I've been having premonitions all my life. Now, I see visions, and they take so much out of me. There's nothing a doctor can do, but I'm so glad you are with me right now.'

'I can stay until I need to get Mollie from school. That gives me an hour. Can I get you anything?'

'Just a glass of water, thank you.'

As Leona recovered, Mona asked, 'Do you want to tell me what happened to you? Maybe I can help?'

'Have you heard of time slips when you see people or places from another time? I don't know if it works in the future, but usually, it's from the past. It could even be a decade ago or much further back in time. When I see these people, they don't engage with me, and I'm not sure if they can see me. They are clearly not wearing modern clothes and are walking about, just getting on with their lives. Don't misunderstand me; I don't think I am seeing ghosts, not in the conventional sense, anyway. This happens away from home as well, in shops, cafes and even in the street. Everything changes as it would have looked then, including buildings, shops and paths.'

'I have heard of time slips, yes. There was a famous case which involved two women; this was in the early years of the twentieth century. They were English but having a holiday in Paris, visiting the Petit Trianon gardens at Versailles on the anniversary of the French Revolution. They saw, amongst others, Marie Antoinette, nobles, gardeners, buildings and paths, which were no longer there at the time of their visit. What were their names now?'

'Moberly and Jourdain,' interrupted Leona, 'an excellent film was made, dealing with their experiences, which I came upon quite by chance. The women's real names were changed, so in the film, they were Miss Morison and Miss Lamont. After seeing it, I bought the book they wrote called "The Adventure", which details the events. Strangely, they didn't see all the things that the other did. Absolutely fascinating. Do you think this might be happening to me?'

'Since knowing you, I've seen and experienced things I never knew were possible, so, yes, I think it is likely.'

'It's good to have a friend, someone I can trust,' answered Leona. 'I've been giving your situation a lot of thought lately. How are things currently at home?'

'It's difficult because Malcolm wants me to stay. He says I'll change my mind, just give it time, and so on and so on, but I know I won't change my mind. Well, I made a mistake, and now, it's up to me to put it right.'

'Have you have any idea how long you might have to wait for a house?'

'I'm not in danger, and I live in a decent place, so I may have to wait some time. I'm not working and only have child benefit so that I will qualify for social housing.'

'Listen to me, Mona. How would you like to move in here? I have plenty of room, two extra bedrooms, and I would love the company. It would help both of us. What do you say?'

'I say it's a wonderful idea. Thank you so much, Leona.'

Mona moved in the next day with Mollie. She left Malcolm a note, saying she had left but would be in touch. He was to contact her if he wanted to see Mollie. They loaded all their personal possessions into Leona's large car. That first evening, when Mollie had gone to bed, the two women talked things over.

'What do you think happened to you yesterday, Leona? I mean, about the vision.'

Leona shook her head. 'I honestly don't know, but it was different. More spiritual, mysterious. It left me bewildered and out of my depth. The light was so bright, almost blinding, but there was also a feeling of deep peace, which I have never felt before.'

'Would you like to have that experience again?'

'Yes, but only in the house. If it happened outside, the results could be devastating. Suppose I was driving, for instance. Still, it's all outside of my control. Tell you what, we'll have a glass or two of wine to toast this new chapter in our lives.'

Mona looked for a job; anything would do. Maybe the pub or the cafe needed staff? Something was bound to come up. Leona felt

good about her decision and was determined to face life with renewed
hope.

CHAPTER SIX

Inevitably, Ethan and Dulap would meet, and just as inevitable that they would form an unbreakable friendship that would change their lives. A stranger meeting them could only form one conclusion: they were father and son because, despite the age difference, the similarity in their appearance was striking. Both were short but strong and wiry, blond hair bleached by the sun, though Ethan wore his short, while Dulap tied his long hair back with a piece of cloth. Both had deep blue eyes. Even the way they walked or stood mimicked the other one. The pair were inseparable, and now, they both walked through the woods and watched Bates and the other gamekeepers.

Dulap had never worked in the normal sense but made his money by using his skills, which were much in demand by farmers and those who had money and couldn't do the work themselves. This included gardening, mending stone walls, hedge laying, thatching and general odd jobs. He met Ethan most days, sometimes camping out. Ethan loved to hear Dulap's stories and experiences, things he had never done but wanted to.

Peter was resentful of the relationship. After all, he was Ethan's father, but despite his efforts to forge a closer bond with his son, he knew he was losing ground to this strange man. That Ethan had no interest in the farm only made his position worse. What was the attraction? Dulap lived in a run-down cottage inherited from his parents. His parentage was also very doubtful. Common gossip said he was the son of a prostitute, father unknown. Did he take drugs? Peter didn't want Ethan to take part in that. What did they talk about when they met all the time? Ethan preferred Dulap's company to his own. Still, he had Mattie; she was still faithful to him and loved the farm. Maybe he should be grateful that at least one of his children wanted to be with him. He should talk to Susan. She must have a view of Dulap. Did she approve of this friendship?

Susan was sympathetic but had a different view of Dulap. She liked him.

' I understand how you feel, Peter, really, I do, but try to see things from Ethan's point of view. He's met someone who is so like himself. He cares about all the same things, and now, Ethan has a proper companion to share his interests and life with. I rather think that neither of us can compete with that, so why not welcome Dulap into the family? That way, you may find favour with Ethan. Anyway, just give it time. You don't want to lose him forever, do you? Actually, I was thinking of inviting Dulap for a meal.'

Peter didn't like it, but he agreed. 'Right, Susan, fine, but don't expect too much from me. I'm doing this for Ethan.'

'Fair enough,' replied Susan, 'but don't spoil things. How old do you think Dulap is? I would say at least mid-sixties; could be older, it's hard to say. I have made a few enquiries about him in the village. As far as I know, he has never been in trouble with the police; well, nothing that they know about, anyway. My feelings are that he will guide and protect Ethan and keep him out of trouble. He's been around for a long time and knows how to take care of himself. He'll care for our son in the same way. Also, he's liked in the area. Don't forget that Ethan's always got his family to turn to, even if he's forgotten that for now.'

'I know you're right, Susan. Anyway, what choice do we have? When were you thinking of having this meal?'

'This Sunday. I don't suppose Dulap's a great churchgoer. I'll talk to Ethan when he comes in.'

Ethan came home in the early evening. Dulap had been teaching him about the different fungi, how to recognise which were poisonous and those which were edible; this had long been part of his foraging life. Ethan learned fast, always taking his notebook and pencil with him. His knowledge of the countryside grew steadily.

'Hello. Ethan,' Susan said, 'supper won't be long now. Mattie's upstairs and your father will be in soon. We wanted to ask you something. Don't worry, it's something nice to look forward to. Sit down, I'll call them.'

Peter started the conversation. 'We know you've made quite a friend of Dulap, Ethan, and we're happy about that. It wasn't good that you were so much on your own before, so we thought it would be nice to invite him to a meal on Sunday and get to know him a bit. There's no ulterior motive, just taking an interest in your life. We all care about you, that's all.'

Ethan was pleased. 'I'll ask him tomorrow. I'm sure he'll come. He enjoys meeting people and is always free on Sunday.'

'Dulap's a funny name,' Mattie said, 'wonder how he came by that?'

'Not sure,' replied Ethan, 'cool name, though; it suits him. He's an unusual person and very interesting. He's lived his life exactly as he wanted to; does nothing unless he knows it's right for him?' Ethan looked at Susan, who felt uncomfortable under his gaze. Did he know about her affair with Jack? Was he criticising her for falling in with Peter's dreams, even though she hadn't wanted it? Well, her life wasn't too bad at the moment, although she missed Jack. Should she contact him? 'That's settled then,' she said, 'Sunday, let's say five.'

The next day, Saturday, Ethan walked out to meet Dulap as usual. The older man was sitting on a wall eating sandwiches. 'Hey, Ethan, want one? Freshly made by me.'

'You enjoy them, Dulap. I'm full of breakfast. Where are we going today?'

'We need to step up the action against Bates. He and his mates are getting ready for the shooting season. There's a crow trap I want to visit. I'm thinking there might be a buzzard in there. If there is, we need to release it before it's battered to death. What do you know about traps, Ethan?'

'I know they are used for controlling covid numbers. I released a magpie from one once.'

'Do you know the difference between a legally operated trap and an illegal one?'

'I'm not sure,' answered Ethan.

'Well, a legal trap should display a sign or a tag with the telephone number of the local police station. The traps operated here try to mislead the public, saying it's part of a bird conservation project. Bates and his cronies don't care about crows; they want to trap and kill raptors like buzzards and owls, and that is illegal. I've seen pigeons and doves used as decoys to trap them, and he didn't release them. Of course, we shouldn't interfere with the traps on this estate, but to hell with that. Bates doesn't play fair, and neither will we. Still, I want you to keep away from gamekeepers, Ethan. Come with me, but do exactly what I say. I've got years of experience dealing with this. Bates won't know we've been anywhere near.'

They reached the grouse moors. Dulap scanned the area through his binoculars and then walked on to an area of rough grass where the trap was.

'See,' explained Dulap, ' a bird, once attracted, enters the trap via a funnel at the top. Once inside, it's impossible to escape unaided. Look here; they have placed a freshly killed rabbit inside to attract maybe a raven or a buzzard. There are several pairs in the area. The law protects these birds. Crouch down in the grass and keep a look-out while I do a bit of damage.'

The door was padlocked, so Dulap took a wire cutter out of his rucksack, destroying one side of the trap. He removed the rabbit, taking it home to cook.

'Now, let's get away from here before we're caught.'

Later that day, Bates discovered the damaged trap, cursing himself for having missed the bastard who had done it. He knew Dulap was making his work more difficult; now he had him and the boy to deal with. Dulap was a seasoned campaigner with an uncanny knack for avoiding him. Still, there was plenty of work to be done with the first shoot not far off. One day soon, he would confront Whottle and when he did...

CHAPTER SEVEN

Jack Field was a lonely man; he regretted his decision to stop seeing Susan. Why had he done it? Guilt? He liked Peter and thought of him as a genuine friend, but did he deserve this amount of loyalty? He knew their marriage was effectively over, and he certainly hadn't caused it. He missed Susan and wanted her back. Peter had gained in confidence as a farmer; in fact, Jack admired him as far as his farming abilities were concerned. Clipping the ewes was imminent and Peter would need his help with that. Jack visited the farm and tried to see Susan.

'Hello, Peter. Just come round to arrange the shearing schedule. Still need my help?'

'Jack, great to see you. We haven't been in contact for a while.' He laughed. 'Have done nothing to offend you, have I? How's everything?'

'Couldn't be better, thanks. I thought you would need a hand with the shearing, like last year. I hired a couple of lads to help me. Mind you, it's expensive that way.'

'That's good of you, Jack. I could do with your help. Go inside for a bit. I'll come in soon, and I'm sure Susan would like to see you.'

Susan was pleased to see Jack again, wondering what it meant; however, she was mad at him for dumping her. 'Hello Jack, what brings you here? You've been a stranger lately.'

'Didn't mean to be, just a lot of work to do at home, that's all. I'm going to help Peter with the shearing soon. One of the hardest jobs I know. When it's done, the ewes will need re-marking again, and the wool needs to be packed up and then sent off.'

'Goodness,' Susan replied sarcastically, 'you'll be around most of the week then? Want a cool beer?'

Susan brought the beers and sat down. 'Stay for the afternoon unless you have anything more pressing to do. In fact, stay for supper. When does shearing start?'

'Thought we'd begin Wednesday... look, Susan, I'm sorry, really sorry, just keeping away and not offering an explanation. I've really missed you. Can we see each other again? Will you come to the farm?'

'I'm hurt, you know, Jack. Did you stop seeing me because of Peter? He's never been aware of our relationship. It wouldn't occur to him. I sometimes wonder if Ethan suspects, though I doubt he would say anything if he did. He might understand. It's lonely for me as well, you know. I see little of Ethan these days. Mattie and I were close, but she's always doing coursework or helping Peter.'

'Sorry, Susan. I suppose I panicked but regretted it almost immediately. Thought you might ring me or come round, but why should you? Give me another chance. I won't mess up again, I promise.'

Susan regarded him for a minute, then smiled, 'I'd like that; I missed you too. I go for a walk most days; the family has got used to my routine, so, shall we say tomorrow, about mid-day? By the way, do you know anyone by the name of Dulap?'

'Dulap Whottle? Yes, of course, everyone does. Why?'

'Ethan's become rather attached to him. Is he trustworthy? Don't want my son to get into any trouble. I met him once when I was having a drink in the pub. He introduced himself. Quite a character, isn't he? Know much about his history?'

'I know he was born in the area; I remember seeing his mother, but his father left when he was a boy. He's unconventional, liked by most people and earns money by doing jobs for people. He's never been in trouble with the law, although I suspect he's guilty of minor infringements for protecting wildlife. The gamekeepers hate him; always complaining about him to the police but without proof. He's a clever man and a decent one too. Don't worry, he'll look after Ethan.'

'He's coming here tomorrow,' Susan replied, 'it will please Ethan and give Peter a chance to get to know him, to get his measure. There's nothing we can do about their friendship, anyway. I think Peter is waiting for you, so I'll come and see you on Monday.'

'Yes, see you then. I'll leave the door unlocked.'

'Bye then, Jack.'

Susan was pleased; this is what she wanted, at least for now. No need for anyone to get hurt; besides, the rest of the family was doing just what they wanted, so she would do the same.

That evening, they were all together. Everyone talked and laughed, happy in each other's company. This is the way it used to be, Susan thought, when they were a proper family. Mattie had done well in her final exams; her relief was obvious. 'I can't believe I've finished them. I honestly didn't think I'd done that well.'

'We never doubted you, Mattie,' Peter said. 'Now you can concentrate on your farming career if that's what you still want to do. No rush; take some time off. You deserve it. Help with the shearing if you want something to do, though. Jack's coming next week to make a start. There's a real skill to this, especially making sure the ewes are not hurt.'

'How's your day been, Ethan?' Susan asked. 'Been out and about with Dulap?'

'Yes, I have. That guy's amazing, Mum. He's looking forward to coming, by the way. He said he'd met you before, in the local pub. Took quite a shine to you; knows where I get my good looks from.'

Susan laughed. 'Indeed, Ethan, he's right. I liked him too; he's a genuine character. I'm looking forward to meeting him again.' She had to admit to herself that the evening was turning into a merry time spent with her family. Even Peter's company was welcome. Susan knew it wouldn't last, and tomorrow, Jack would once more assume his rightful place in her life.

Dulap arrived with Ethan, determined to make a good impression, wearing carefully pressed, grey corduroy trousers, a fresh shirt under his familiar faded waistcoat, carrying flowers and an expensive bottle of wine. Peter had forced himself to attend, having grave concerns about the influence of this man on Ethan. Rumours had recently reached him about some damage to a crow trap; of course, Dulap was responsible for this and no doubt Ethan had been with him. Peter felt uncomfortable, but he would try to get on with this man. Dulap omitted having met Susan previously, for which she was grateful; it showed a sensitivity she had not expected. Mattie took an immediate liking for Ethan's new friend; he was not the country "numpty" she had expected him to be. He was intelligent and strangely interesting. Dulap expressed an interest in the farm, which pleased Peter, who asked Dulap about himself.

'I had no formal training growing up, but there's always something I can turn my skills to. Folks always need help with all kinds of jobs; a bit of D.I. Y, gardening, repairs. I'm an expert with hedge laying and dry stone walling. I get by and earn enough for my daily needs. You get the picture.'

'Yes,' replied Peter, 'I hear you're concerned about hunting and shooting. You don't agree with that, then?'

'Well, no, that's accurate enough, but it's the illegal goings-on that I am compelled to do something about. You understand that, Peter?'

'I do, but do you break the law in order to achieve it?'

Dulap smiled and said, 'Only when the law's broken by others who should know better. There needs to be harsher punishments for landowners and gamekeepers; then I wouldn't have to step in and interfere.'

Susan interrupted, 'Can this conversation take place at a different time, please? Let's enjoy the meal and each other's company for now.'

The atmosphere became lighter; Dulap asked Peter to show him around the farm, after which they all sat in the garden, enjoying the rest of the afternoon. Susan was proud of her work here, having transformed it by cleverly using wild plants and traditional cottage flowers together. Common toadflax, teasels, horned poppies, foxes and cubs grew alongside Canterbury bells, hollyhocks and delphiniums, pink and blue.

'Where do you live, Dulap?' Mattie asked.

'I live in the middle of a wood, in an old cottage made for those who worked on the land years back. Modernised since then, of course, Mattie. A solid cottage with a good-sized garden. I grow most of my vegetables and fruit there, like a small allotment, really. Come and visit me whenever I'm home. Do lots of baking, too. Don't get many visitors, except for Ethan. He tells me you're taking up farming like your dad. Not an easy life, a rewarding one if you've a mind. Take Jack Field, for example; born into it, he was and kept going despite many setbacks. Decent chap, Jack. Helps you a lot, Peter, so I hear?'

Susan felt her cheeks burning. Does Dulap know about her and Jack? No doubt he's seen her going to Jack's farm. Not a man to make an enemy of, that's for sure.

'Yes,' Peter answered, 'Jack's a good friend. I'd never have survived without his help. He's helping me with the annual shearing, starting Tuesday. I respect the way he handles the ewes, when I watched him shear his own last week.'

'Well, I'll be going now. I've had a great time; thank you all for inviting me. Let me know if you need extra help with the shearing. Will you see me to the road, Ethan?'

'Yes, sure.'

'I thought that went well,' Susan said, 'I would say that Ethan's in safe hands with Dulap. Don't you think so, Peter?'

Peter shrugged. 'Yes, I suppose he's basically sound, but he can't be looking out for Ethan all the time. After all, we still don't know who attacked Bates; Dulap must be the prime suspect, even if the police can't pin anything on him. Bates accused Ethan, remember? That he's made such a friend of Dulap will only make things worse.'

'Yes, I see your point. Still, what can we do? We can hardly forbid our son from seeing him. Anyway, I'm going to clear away now and wash up.'

Ethan walked partway to Dulap's home. 'You have a delightful family, Ethan. I never had that kind of family life; I envy you.'

'I don't think my parents' marriage is all that great. They put on an act because you were coming round.'

'Sorry to hear that, Ethan. Still, I'm glad I met them; Mattie too.'

CHAPTER EIGHT

July swept into August, and a breath of summer lingered on. Red berries were forming on the mountain ash, and in the hedgerows, the elder flowers turned into the fruits so loved by birds. Hazels created an abundance of nuts, while conkers grew on the horse chestnuts. The virginia creeper, growing against cottage walls, now burst into flames, and there was an unmistakable autumn feel to the mornings, with a freshness in the air, although the creeping hands of early frosts had not yet trapped the remaining vegetables not collected from the allotments.

Now, with the summer moult behind them, the many varieties of birds could find food in the hedgerows and the gardens, attracted by seed hoppers and strings of peanuts. Some began singing; the melodic repetition of the song thrush, the robin's metallic trill. A few swallows and house martins lingered on, perched on wires and cables, but as the year progressed, struggling against the rough and chilly winds, they caught the last of the insects and prepared to leave.

There is a period in August when the summer sun can no longer dry the hidden dew, sheltered in the long grass. Then, at last, summer must give up its sovereignty to autumn. A sunny afternoon still tempted out butterflies, such as peacocks and red admirals, which hovered to feed on the last of the summer flowers.

Mona loved this time of year, looking forward to the cooler weather, perhaps long-awaited rain and the cosy feel of autumn, with shorter days. She watched the robins chasing each other about the garden, the young ones beginning to produce their red breasts and being chased out of the territory by the parents in quarrelsome disputes. Goldfinches twitted as they picked out seeds from the thistles and teasel heads. Above all, she loved to hear the rooks, feeding on the abundance of insect grubs and worms, then rising as a flock, suddenly swooping downwards, cawing and flying up again to settle on their nests once more.

Towards the third week, with the emergence of the craneflies or "daddy longlegs", the rooks were busily feeding on the pupae in gardens and fields. Wood pigeons, settling in the large trees within gardens, gorged themselves on acorns and cooed in the branches.

The beginning of August had been warm and calm, the air filled with the last of the insects, with aphids seeking somewhere to lay their eggs before dying. House sparrows, chaffinches and starlings dashed about, trying to catch all they could.

Mona had made it one of her jobs to keep the feeding stations well stocked. Sometimes, black-headed gulls flew back and forth, twisting and turning, seeing if they could take bigger morsels from the bird table. Occasionally, a male sparrow hawk swept down, having flown along the line of the hedge, trying to catch a small bird.

This morning, Mona went for a walk. It had been misty, but now a soft haze covered the features of the landscape. The ivy was in flower, attracting drone flies and bluebottles. Trees were colouring, birch and hazel were getting ready to shed their orange and yellow leaves. She startled a pheasant, which rose, whirring away from her, then gliding with down-turned wings and a loud 'korr-kok'. Here and there, Mona noticed trees which were barren stumps, or uprooted by the fierce winds of previous years. The first fieldfares and redwings were seen in the fields, winter visitors heralding the start of autumn.

Mona wandered into a small wood she had visited before, looking for fungi, especially her favourite, the white agarics, growing on thin white stalks, gathered around hazel stools. She halted. Was that a bullfinch? A glimpse of white rump disappearing into the hedge and a soft indrawn whistle. It was gone.

Coming out of the wood brought her to the lane again, which led to the church. She tried the church door. It opened. The air was cool, with a whiff of incense.

She realised she was not on her own. A young man, tall, with thick black hair was walking towards her. The most noticeable thing about him were his eyes; large, pale blue, enlarged by his glasses. Mona felt uncomfortable under his gaze.

'Hello, welcome to St. Margaret's. It's an old church, some of it dating back to Anglo-Saxon times. There are leaflets on the table. Please take one.' He moved away, and then, much to Mona's annoyance, he came back.

'Are you new to the village or just a visitor? I don't remember seeing you before.'

Mona smiled a little. 'Yes, I've lived here for a while now but never walked this way before. I like to visit churches. I share a house with Leona, the clairvoyant and my daughter, Mollie. Perhaps you've heard of my friend?'

The minister nodded. 'Yes, I know who she is. I believe she's made quite a name for herself, especially with the local women, who seem to need her services.'

'She's well known outside of the village too,' replied Mona. 'I expect you don't approve of what she does?'

'Indeed, I don't. The Church usually frowns on such practices. However, I don't believe your friend can have any genuine powers. Do you think she does?'

'I admit I was sceptical myself at first,' replied Mona, 'but now I know she has a genuine gift. She is also the kindest person I have ever met. She has given Mollie and myself a home when we desperately needed somewhere to live. And I can tell you this. Leona pays a heavy price for what she does, suffering herself when she must tell a client bad news. Many a time, they blame her but she only tells them the truth. If you knew her, you would see what a lovely person she is.'

Mona walked out of the church without another word, closing the door behind her with relief; she walked a little further before turning for home. Rooks were going to their nightly roosts, three ancient, tall trees on the edge of the wood. They circled around in fast, wide circles, in quiet, restless flight or sailing the wildly buffeted winds, which were becoming increasingly rainy. Mona sensed the changing season and the end of summer. In the morning, the birds would return to their feeding grounds, but tonight, they huddled together, black shapes safe in the wildest of weathers.

Mona hardly knew where she was or where she was going. She had been wandering for about forty minutes and knew it was time to turn back. Suddenly, the road turned into a narrow pathway. There were trees on both sides, some oak, others silver birch and limes. They weren't displaying much autumn colour, just a few leaves which were bright yellow, turning brown. The older of the trees were huge, with low branches, many bent, thick and twisted. Mona noticed the tall, spreading tops, the centres of which were filled with mistletoe.

The path petered out, revealing a clearing and a small cottage, whitewashed and in need of some repair. There were several big wire cages and pens, all with roosting boxes, perches and water. In one, a female sparrowhawk sat and stared at her.

'Hello, welcome to my place. I'll show you around if you care to.'

Startled, Mona spun around, so quickly that she nearly lost her footing. 'Oh, I didn't mean to trespass. I seem to have lost my way when I came off the main path. Could you give me directions back; I need to get to the church. I know where to go from there. It's getting dark, and I need to get home.'

'No problem. My name's Dulap, by the way. I'll show you a quick way to the village so that you can orientate yourself.'

Within twenty minutes, she was back home. Mollie and Leona were pleased and relieved to see her.

'Thank goodness you're back, Mona. Mollie and I were getting worried, haven't we, Mollie?'

'Mummy, where have you been?'

'Sorry, darling; I got a bit lost; silly me. I met a nice man who lives in a cottage in the middle of a wood. He's got a funny name, Dulap. Do you know about him, Leona?'

'I do,' replied Leona, 'at least, by reputation. What was he like?'

'An interesting man, although I only met him briefly. Dulap rescues birds, especially birds of prey, and told me they were persecuted on the moors and in the woods; he doesn't like gamekeepers very much. Told me all about it when he was showing me a way to the village. He's really very hidden away. I think he's someone you really like or prefer to avoid. I belong to the former. Thanks for collecting Mollie, Leona.'

'It's a pleasure. I've been helping Mollie with her homework, and it's all done.'

'Yes, Mummy, Leona's really helped me. We've had a lovely time, although we both missed you, of course.'

Mollie went upstairs to play, which gave Leona a chance to speak to Mona.

'What a delightful child Mollie is; I have become so fond of you both. Not having any children of my own, it's like having a daughter and a granddaughter. Anyway, I've been giving our situation some thought. The only living relatives I have are a couple of nephews, which I haven't seen in years. They disapproved of my "gift", and I'm unlikely to see either of them again. I have, therefore changed my will, leaving the house and any money I have to you. You and Mollie will then be secure. Of course, you don't have to remain living here to inherit from me; that is entirely up to you. Wait—say nothing yet.

Let me explain something to you first. I had a sister, but she died when I was only ten. She was never a sturdy child, but my mother blamed herself for Wanda's death; I miss her and feel her near me often. So, you see, Mona, it would make me very happy if you would accept my offer.'

Mona listened intently to Leona; her kindness and generosity overwhelmed her. She could only thank her, assuring her friend that she and Mollie already called the house their home.

'That's as it should be.' Leona continued, 'I knew from our first meeting that you would both become important to me. Remember that day when you stood outside my door, not knowing what to do? It must have been fate that brought you to me then. But Mona, there is something else which I must talk to you about. There is a big change coming to my life, and there is absolutely nothing I can do about it. I am going to need your support and strength more than ever. Don't be afraid of what you may see or experience. There is no risk to you or Mollie.'

'You're worrying me, Leona,' Mona said, 'but I promise I will be there for you no matter what happens. Just tell me what I must do. What is this change?'

'I'm not sure myself,' Leona answered, 'but afterwards, I will need to rest, enter a new life, to be free. Now, I think Mollie needs you upstairs. Go to her, and I'll start supper. Nothing will happen tonight; the signs will make themselves known soon. Just stay with me when the time comes. Honestly, it really isn't something you need to worry about.'

Mona went upstairs, wondering what all this could mean. This must have something to do with the visions Leona had been experiencing. Yes, that was surely it. She occupied herself with giving Mollie a bath, before supper.

Mollie was the only one who slept well that night. Mona lay awake, trying to understand what was happening to her friend. Sleep evaded Leona, too; the headaches had become worse lately. Had she read the signs correctly, or was she mistaken? Was it an illness, something that could be treated medically? No, she was sure that whatever was happening to her was inevitable and beyond her control; It would make itself known before long.

CHAPTER NINE

This was a big day for Ethan. He would wait for Dulap, ready for whatever his friend had planned, and he didn't want to let him down. He carefully laid his belongings on the bed to make sure he had forgotten nothing. Notebook, pens, a flask of tea and plastic cups, sandwiches, bottles of water, hand wipes, gloves and a hat. The binoculars he wore around his neck. Satisfied everything was in order, he packed them into his rucksack and went downstairs. Good, no one was up yet. His phone was safely in his jacket pocket. Ethan still preferred to wear a watch to check the time; ten to five, he could easily walk to the meeting place in good time.

While he waited for Dulap, Ethan considered the day ahead. His companion wanted to check the burial site of a pair of short-eared owls, probably buried at the bottom of a dry stone wall. To reach the spot, they would have to walk over part of the moors, which was private land. The plan was not to remove them but to take photos and record the incident, then report the crime in the hope of a prosecution.

Dulap walked up to Ethan without him realising.

'Hey, you'll have to be sharper than this, Ethan; I could have been Bates. The trick is to keep relaxed but always aware of your surroundings and ready to get away as quickly as possible. Check for the best entrances and escape routes.'

'Sorry, Dulap, I was thinking about the day ahead, trying to prepare myself. I know this could be an important day in the fight against Bates.'

Dulap laughed. 'Didn't mean to be sharp. Stick with me, and you'll be fine. I know you can find your way around. You've been doing all right before we met. It's just that I have a duty to you and to your family to keep you safe. Right, let's go.'

As always, they went through the woods. The trees afforded protection and camouflage as they approached the edge of the moors. Dulap had previously cut a section of the wire; they stepped out and crouched down, scanning the moors with their binoculars.

'Well,' Dulap said, 'we seem to have the place to ourselves, lad. So, let's hurry. I'm pretty sure I know where the owls are, so follow me.'

It didn't take long to cover the area of heather scrub, reaching the stone wall in five minutes. They could see an empty jeep, which was a worry, but they saw no one.

'Keep low, Ethan. We need to move along the wall, further up this way. Yes, there it is. You can see where the stones have been moved and not replaced very well. I'll just take these away and, yes, as I thought, two owls, shot in the air and then stuffed in here.'

Dulap laid the two corpses together and took several pictures with his small camera. 'I know I could use my phone, but habits die hard, and I've always done it this way. Now, I'll put them back as best I can, then we should get back to the woods.'

'Got you, you bastard. I thought you might show up. Oh, got your little helper with you today I see.' Roger Bates stood on the other side of the wall with a rifle pointed at them.

'O.K. Bates,' shouted Dulap, 'why don't you put the rifle down? If you want a fight, you can have one. I know what you've done, and I've got the evidence. You'll not get away with it this time.'

Bates sneered. 'You can't prove anything unless you saw me kill the birds and then put them in the wall. Get the hell out of here before I use this.'

'Come on, Ethan, he's all bluff. Let's go. I've got what I wanted. We'll go somewhere else and eat our sandwiches; I could do with a cup of tea as well. I can see you're a bit shaken. It isn't every day you face an angry gamekeeper with a rifle. He's gone now. Best not to tell your parents about this, but I'm happy to tell them myself if that's what you want.'

'No, of course not, Dulap. Bates doesn't scare me; I've had run-ins with him before. I admit I was frightened, but, as you say, we have the proof. That's what we came for.'

They found a fallen log in the woods, where a small patch of sunlight still penetrated through the canopy. The sandwiches and hot tea had the effect of bringing the morning's events back to normality. The trees surrounding them seemed to comfort and protect them.

'I'll go to the police station in the morning,' Dulap said, 'see what they have to say about it. I'm annoyed with myself because today, I let my guard down. Normally, Bates could never get that close. After all, I had seen the vehicle, so the chances of someone being near were high. He just wanted to frighten us,'

'I understand, Dulap, really I do. It was rather exciting, in a way. I come out with you because I want to make a difference, it's worth the risk. The main thing is, you have the photos.'

They went back to Dulap's cottage. The sparrowhawk was healing well. Dulap promised Ethen he would be there when she flew.

It was midday when Ethan returned home. Peter was sweeping the yard. He waved at his son. 'Been out with Dulap? Had a good time?'

'Yes, dad, he's looking after a sparrowhawk, which he's going to set free soon. I've never been so close to one. A female too, bigger than the male.'

'That's great, Ethan. He seems like a nice man, genuine if you know what I mean. I'll finish up here and come in for a bit.'

Mattie was watching television in the sitting room while Susan was looking at the morning papers. She looked up.

'Hello, Ethan, want something to eat?'

'No thanks, mum. I shared something with Dulap. I'll have a coffee, though.'

'Right you are. Where have you been this morning? I'm not checking up on you, by the way. Just interested, that's all. I'll make the coffee.'

'That's o.k, Mum. We just went for a walk. Then went back to his cottage for a while. It's nice there. Looked at an injured sparrowhawk. She will fly soon.'

'That's nice. I'd like to see her myself. Perhaps you could ask Dulap for me.'

Peter came in. 'Any coffee going? Jack's visiting later. Nothing specific. I just think he wants company. It must be quite lonely for him sometimes. I said he could stay for supper.'

'Yes, of course he can.' Susan felt her face blushing, hoping no one noticed. Just the mention of Jack's name excited her, but for how much longer, she couldn't say. Anyway, it would be nice to have the family and Jack sitting around the kitchen table later on.

The daylight faded much earlier now, and the atmosphere seemed damp-laden; the birds had stopped singing. In the mornings, frosts touched everything, although for a day or two, the sun still managed a few sun-light hours.

Mona stood in the garden as dusk approached, watching a flock of starlings, each individual bird manoeuvring into an entire flock like a cloud. Then, drifting into a tree to roost. Gregarious lapwings were feeding in the fields, walking in organised lines, while the rooks spiralled and twisted from the fields to their high roosts.

She looked up at Leona's window. The curtains were not quite closed, and a light shone from the bedside table. She had taken to going to bed earlier, seeming to need the rest and quiet. Mona walked Mollie to and from school but was never away from the house for long. She remembered her meeting with Dulap and wondered if she could engineer another one. Just why she wanted to see him again, she couldn't say, but he was certainly someone of interest to her. She had to admit to an attraction to this strange man and smiled to herself.

Bates was feeling very pleased with himself. What a performance he had given. It was the first time he had ever got one over on that old sod, Dulap Whottle. Maybe the bugger was losing his touch. There was no proof that he had shot those bloody owls; no one saw him do it. Then, a doubt touched him. How did Whottle know where he'd hidden them? Maybe he'd filmed him, in which case he had to get hold of his camera. Well, no point worrying about that now. He doubted there was much the police could do, anyway. Still, he'd better be on his guard. Remembering his attack, it could well have been Dulap.

Dulap sat in his cottage, planning his next move. He had seen Bates with the owls, but his film was inconclusive. He had simply been too far away, but of course, Bates didn't know that. The gamekeeper was no easy adversary. He would have to unsettle Bates; follow and watch him, let the gamekeeper see him. Eventually, Bates would slip up, and when he did...

CHAPTER TEN

Mattie was very unhappy. She could not say exactly when her moods altered; it was a slow, inevitable change which she was incapable of stopping. Throughout her senior years at school, she had been the most content and happy girl, seeing her future positively. She would take her final exams and progress to agricultural college to work full-time on the farm. Any other career was not to be considered. Having made this decision, she helped Peter whenever she could, taking pride in her work and gaining knowledge and experience.

She knew her father had problems, making mistakes, which were costly. He struggled to complete all his tasks, and his health was not as it had been. Without her and Jack's help, it was doubtful whether the farm would survive at all. Peter depended on her; now, she was letting him down. Mattie couldn't understand herself; how could she have been so certain and now question everything? She felt lost. Maybe it was a matter of giving herself time and taking advice on what to do. She would talk to her mother; Ethan was out of the question. Yes, he would listen to her, but she doubted he would be of any real help. Susan knew Mattie was unhappy. This afternoon, mother and daughter sat down together.

'Right, darling, talk to me. Be honest and tell me how you are feeling.'

'I'm just not sure about taking the agricultural option, Mum. I haven't applied yet and can't bring myself to do so. Worse than that though, I don't enjoy working on the farm, like I used to do. I just feel terrible.'

Susan reflected. 'Why don't you take some time off; forget about college for the time being. You're young and have time for all that in the future; see how you feel a year from now. You may have a clearer idea of how to proceed with your life. Of course, I shall have to talk to your dad. Are you saying you don't want to help him anymore?'

'Yes, please talk to him. He's going to be really disappointed, isn't he?'

'Of course,' replied Susan, 'but he knew the risks when he bought the farm. I thought it foolish, watching him struggling; sometimes, he comes in absolutely exhausted. Other mornings, he's late milking the cows, and that puts him out for the rest of the day. But, Mattie, that's not your problem. You can talk to him yourself if you want; tell him how you're feeling. I think he will understand. But, if you don't want to do that, it's fine.'

Two days passed. Mattie kept mostly to her bedroom, resting or reading. She had kept a journal of her day-to-day moods and her thoughts. She had read somewhere that it was a useful aid when feeling down. Susan made an appointment to take Mattie to the doctor, as she felt she had depression. Peter missed her companionship and talked to Susan about her.

'Mattie hasn't been working on the farm lately. Of course, she doesn't have to, but she always did so willingly, and I've missed her. What's wrong, Susan? I know something is. It's not healthy, spending all day in her bedroom, never going out.'

'I wanted Mattie to talk to you herself, Peter, and she feels bad about letting you down. It's clear to me she's depressed and needs some kind of help. We had a talk about how she feels. She's reconsidering her future, not sure farming is what she wants to do. College is out of the question, at least for now. We'll help her all we can, but you will just have to manage the farm on your own, with Jack's help, of course.'

Peter was clearly upset but at a loss how to respond. Instead, he returned to the yard. Susan thought he looked small and frail. Certainly not the man she had married.

At least Ethan was happy. He didn't have coherent plans for his future either; in fact he seemed to drift, but at least he was happy, whatever he was doing each day. What that might be, Susan didn't know, just that it had something to do with his friend, Dulap.

It was quite mild. Even at this time of the year, bulbs had pushed up green-pointed wedges to the surface. Violets and primroses still grew in sheltered places underneath bushes, out of the November winds. Susan left the claustrophobic atmosphere of the kitchen, walking onto the road, taking a turn onto a public footpath through a small coppice, where small birds kept her company. Long-tailed tits flittered from tree to tree with short, restless flights, while blue tits and coal tits performed acrobatic feats on the bare, outstretched twigs.

She found another path, deciding to explore. This ran past a wide brook. Stopping to look in the water, she noticed the purple loosestrife and yellow flag were now dead and brown. All seemed lifeless here until a water rat suddenly splashed into the water, startling her. Lower down, the stream entered a small, boggy copse with elders standing in marshy pools. Susan looked up to the top of the trees. Siskins were extracting seeds from the cones. In the encroaching dusk, a song thrush poured out its lovely song.

Susan felt a sudden panic; she wanted to leave this lonely place and get back home despite all the troubles there.

Mattie had agreed to see a doctor. She prescribed a low dosage of antidepressants and talked to her for some time. She would refer her to a counsellor if Mattie wanted, someone who wasn't involved and with whom she could talk freely, in confidence. Mattie said she would think about it.

One consequence of Peter now working on his own was that Jack came to the farm more often. Peter was finding things difficult now and welcomed Jack's input. The last thing Susan wanted was for Peter to find out about her relationship with Jack. They must be careful.

After a few days of rain and stormy weather, the sun filtered its rays weakly through the clouds; the sky turned a hazy blue. Rabbits sat on banks, taking advantage of the light during milder evenings. Holly bushes offered their red berries to the birds, and Susan brought some in to brighten the window sills. The sunsets during the week were a flaming red before turning deep orange, heralding the first frosts. Trees now stood stark and almost leafless, while the wild clematis, or old man's beard, produced masses of fluffy, white seeds in the hedges. Rooks and jackdaws visited the garden now, along with black-headed gulls, which sailed over the land looking for scraps. Fieldfare populations had increased, moving with the typical hop of the thrush. Starlings fed noisily, running back and forth, squabbling over food.

With Jack's next visit, Susan put an idea to him. Jack sensed Susan's anxious state and asked, 'What's wrong, Susan? What's going on?'

'Peter's overworked, Jack. He's clearly ill. He must get well, but to do that he needs complete rest; stop working for a while. I believe he's brought the cows inside, but I don't know what else needs doing.'

'I'll tell you what, Susan. All my jobs are more or less finished at home, so why don't I move in here? I can manage both farms for a while.'

'Thank you, Jack,' Susan replied, 'I really appreciate it. Just keep things ticking over. You'll have to sleep on the sofa, I'm afraid, but it's really very comfortable. I'm worried about Mattie, too. She's depressed; I'm at a loss to know what to do. She's lost all interest in the farm, which came as a real shock, especially to Peter. Ethan's the only one who's happy. He's always out with Dulap; I don't know where he goes, but he returns late every afternoon, glad enough to be home.'

'Taken up with Dulap, has he?' Jack laughed. 'He's a nice enough chap; unconventional, that's all. There is one thing you should know, though. He's got some issues with Roger Bates, the gamekeeper on the estate. There have been one or two incidents between the two. Bates is a dangerous man to meddle with.'

Susan nodded. 'Do you remember when Bates was attacked earlier in the year? Bates accused Ethan, but of course there was no proof he had anything to do with it. I worry Dulap is leading Ethan into potential danger. Maybe he was the person who accosted Bates?'

'I don't remember Dulap being around at the time,' Jack answered, 'but who knows? Anyway, we must concentrate on getting Peter well. I'll come back early tomorrow with my things. In the meantime, will you talk to him?'

'Yes, leave it to me, Jack. I'll feel a lot better with you here.'

Susan went to find Peter. She found him slumped on a hay bale in the cowshed, asleep.

'Peter, wake up. Come inside. I need to speak to you, and no arguments, please.'

Peter was in no state to argue. He hadn't realised how cold he was, and hungry too.

'Sit by the fire, Peter. Fancy staying out so long and becoming so cold. Didn't you think to wear your warm jacket? What were you thinking? Now listen to me and don't interrupt because there are going to be major changes, at least for the foreseeable future. You are not fit to work on the farm; you are clearly unwell, and if you carry on as you are, you could become seriously ill. As of tomorrow, Jack is going to live here and take care of things. If he needs help, I can step in. Yes, I can see you're surprised, but I need to do whatever I can to keep this family together. I don't know how to help Mattie at the moment; she's depressed and won't be any help. Ethan will look after himself; I just hope he will keep out of trouble. I will just have to trust him. So, Peter, are you going to be sensible? I want you to rest, keep warm and get well. Then, we will have to talk about the future. I'll bring some soup for you. Will you eat that?'

Peter didn't argue. He knew Susan was right. In fact, he felt an enormous relief, happy to let her take charge. He ate his soup, had a bath and went to bed. Jack would be here in the morning, so, no need to get up early. What a wonderful friend Jack was. Someone he could rely on, someone he could trust.

Susan returned to the warmth of the living room fire. She had seen Peter struggling for months now, even with Mattie's help. Maybe this was the end of Peter's dream of owning a farm. He had tried so hard to make a go of it; now it had come to this. Maybe it was time to sell up and move on, but to what? She looked at the sofa. Unfortunately, Jack would have to sleep there and not with her. Still, it was comfortable. He'd be fine.

Mattie came downstairs. 'Where's Dad? Is he still outside? It's almost dark.'

'No, he's in bed, Mattie. Your Dad isn't well, and he's doing no more work until he's fit to do so. Jack's going to move in for a while to keep things going. I know the animals are the primary concern, and I'll help whenever I can, so don't worry. Anyway, how are you feeling?'

'I just feel so down, Mum.'

'Would you say that you're depressed? Are you still taking the medicine? Of course, it will help, but we need to get to the underlying courses. There's soup if you fancy it. I can quickly heat it up.'

Mother and daughter ate together, enjoying each other's company, as they used to do. Ethan came back. Susan noticed his face was flushed; he seemed excited, animated even. He said nothing and went to his room.

The next morning, Susan was up early, before Jack's arrival. She could hear Peter coughing. Jack arrived shortly after, carrying a suitcase. Susan laughed and said, ' I can see you mean business, Jack. I think you will be here for some time.' She hugged him, feeling his presence such a comfort.

'How are things?' Jack asked. 'Did you speak to Peter?'

'Yes, I did. At least I talked, and Peter listened, and we came to an understanding. To be honest, his compliance surprised me. He was in bed early, and he's still there, nursing a nasty cough and, I suspect, a temperature, too. I'll take a cup of tea up to him in a bit and see how he is.'

'Good, and when you do, I'll have a cup too. Then, I'll go out and see what needs doing.'

'You'll have to sleep on the sofa,' Susan said, 'but it's really comfy. Put your case in my room. You know where everything is, so make yourself at home. Oh, Jack, I'm so glad you're here. What would I, or any of us, do without you?'

'I'm always here for you, Susan if you want me to be.' Jack opened his arms to her. They couldn't resist a kiss.

There were footsteps on the top of the stairs, making the couple move away from each other quickly. Susan looked round, but whoever had been there had gone back upstairs.

CHAPTER ELEVEN

In the few weeks leading up to Christmas, uncommon events occurred, which affected the lives of quite a few residents in the village. Bates was one of these. On a chilly morning, after a hard frost, the gamekeeper made his usual rounds of the moors. After parking his land rover, near the track leading to the gate, he re-filled the game bird's ground feeders, checked the water and then made his way slowly back by walking around the perimeter of the land. As he got closer to the entrance, he could see there was something wrong with his car. The boot was wide open, some windows were smashed, and maybe, yes, one of the back tyres was slashed. Within minutes, he was looking at a badly damaged and burgled vehicle. Checking the boot first, he knew that the tools, which he used as part of his job, were gone. Worse than that, two peregrine eggs, which he wanted to sell via the illegal egg-collecting fraternity, had disappeared, along with a rifle. Whoever had done this had two purposes in mind: to vandalise the land rover and collect evidence, which could lead to a prosecution against him.

Bates phoned the police station.

He had to wait for an hour, which did nothing to improve his temper.

'About time too! Just look at the state of my land rover. It's going to take thousands to put it right.'

Constable Perkins made an initial report of the damage and asked if anything was missing.

'Yes, an expensive rifle. I keep it in the boot when I don't need to use it. Everything else seems to be there,' Bates lied.

Constable Perkins nodded. 'You will need to file a report; then you can get the land rover towed away. I suppose you have suitable insurance cover, Mr Bates?'

'No worries there,' Bates replied, 'my employers will see to that. One perk of the job. I know who did this, and I want him arrested. Dulap Whottle's his name.'

'You saw him by the car, did you, sir? We can't go around arresting people without proof.' Bates wasn't in any mood to accept this question. He bridled, his face reddened. 'Of course, I didn't see him; the old bugger's clever. I don't know how he does it, but it was him all right. He's always on the moors, watching and waiting for any opportunity to stop me from doing my job. He must have been the one who attacked me, then he destroyed a crow trap and now my land rover.'

The constable contradicted the gamekeeper. 'You accused that lad, Ethan, at the time of your attack, Mr Bates, but you don't know who it was, and there's nothing the police can do without proof, as I keep telling you. Now, I suggest you come with me to the station and report the vandalism. You will need a crime number and details to give to the insurance company. Someone will talk to Mr Whottle, but apart from that, as things stand, there is little more we can do. Please don't take the law into your own hands, otherwise, you could get yourself into trouble.'

In another part of the village, Leona was walking alone. Picking up a stout stick on the way, she followed a public footpath she hadn't seen before. Everything seemed bathed in a strange mist; a strong wind had suddenly come, blowing her hair about and tearing at her clothes. She put the hood of her coat over her head, finding gloves in her pocket. They were soft, green and warm. She stroked her face with them, feeling comfort from their contact. Pausing, a thin vile of sun had found its way to where she was standing. The bitter days were lengthening; there were signs that the ancient earth was waking up, though maybe prematurely. A few excited partridges flew from the edge of a field and raced over the recently ploughed fallows.

The wind stopped. The late afternoon sky became white and hazy. Perhaps it would snow tonight, Leona thought. She had entered a strange wood, hushed and quiet. Surely, this was the place she had heard about, the area locals preferred to avoid. Sometimes, the trees were definitely hostile, seeing a human presence as an unwelcome intrusion. On those days they seemed to hang down, closing up the spaces between them, making walking difficult, brambles and nettles slashing at legs and hands.

Today, they welcomed Leona. The wood opened up, eager to show her their secrets. She sat down on a large grassy log, by patches of mushrooms and wildflowers, which should have retreated into the earth months ago. Two figures came into view. Whether they were real or imaginary, Leona couldn't tell, but their appearance brought great contentment, and she rose to greet them. As they parted, a light surrounded them, and a much-loved person came into view: her mother. A smile and a brief embrace and the vision faded, replaced by a man which she knew, but had never seen before. Leona looked into his eyes, which looked deeply into hers; then he was gone. She found her way back home, but at a loss to describe how she got there. Glad to find the house empty, she lay on her bed, closing her eyes, sinking into herself.

When Mona and Mollie came back, Leona wasn't sure what to tell them. She waited until Mollie was in bed and then told her friend what had happened to her. Leona knew that Mona completely accepted her story; she was thankful.

'What a wonderful experience for you, Leona. I have to admit I envy you a little. How do you feel now?'

Leona sighed. ' I have been blessed, Mona. Now, my powers will fade, but I don't mind. In fact, I welcome my freedom, which has become a burden to me. I can truly live my life now as I want to. Of course, some of my clients will be disappointed, but, you know, they never really needed me. Now, we must find some way to celebrate: you, me and Mollie.'

The doorbell rang, making the women jump. Len Crabtree stood in the doorway, asking forgiveness over his anger towards Leona, after she had given his wife, Dawn, a reading. 'Please, come in, Mr Crabtree,' Leona said.

'No,' replied the man, 'I just wanted to apologise, that's all. I know now that you meant no harm to Dawn or to the baby she was carrying. Since then, she has given birth to a healthy boy.'

'I'm so happy for you both. I caused some distress to Dawn and to you too. Anyway, my clairvoyant days are over now. There will be no more readings of any kind. Please give my love to Dawn.'

It snowed during the night; in the morning, a bright sun lit up its pure whiteness. Birds were caught out, with several flying about, not sure where to locate food, trying to find a twig or any spot where the thaw had started, with the rise in temperature. Song thrushes were looking for snails, which harboured in the hedge bottoms, and in the fields, fieldfares, redwings and the occasional Mistle Thrush sought berries from the hawthorn and holly bushes. Everywhere, there were tiny tracks; some made by mice, others, larger ones, by water rats, making a living by the river banks. Grey squirrels left their mark as they visited stores of beech nuts, their prints showing long, slender toes and nails. A stoat had flushed some rabbits out of their burrows amongst the bramble bushes, while in the sky, a kestrel quartered its patch, trying to catch songbirds, its usual prey being scarce. Goldfinches darted about, twittering and scattering the snow from teasels and thistle heads as they fed. Finding shelter from the barren woods, woodcocks retreated to running ditches and drains.

The thaw continued during the morning. Mona added suet, currants, cooked potato and nuts to the seed mixture all ready on the bird table. Mollie helped her. 'I wish the snow hadn't gone, Mummy.'

'Yes,' answered Mona, 'when the snow first falls, it's so magical. The sun makes it really sparkly. All those individual snowflakes are unique; all different, so beautiful, with their intricate lace-work designs. Maybe there will be more snow.'

Mollie was thinking about something else just then. She said, 'I think Leona is much happier than she used to be. Don't you think so, Mummy?'

'Why do you think that, darling?'

'Well,' Mollie said slowly, 'when all those people came to see her, it often made her unhappy. I used to wish they would go away and never come again. I know they have stopped now, but I don't understand why Leona saw them before when it made her feel so sad?'

Mona hugged Mollie and said, 'You noticed all that, and I never knew. You are a very perceptive child. Anyway, Leona won't be sad anymore. She has a special gift that she was born with, like her mother. She could read signs and knew things before they happened. She didn't always get everything right; few people are as perfect as that, but most of the time, she got things spot on. Telling clients nice things was simple, but when she saw bad things, she had to decide whether to tell them. We all have different degrees of mental strength; sometimes people can't bear to hear bad news and would be unhappy. I expect you sometimes saw them crying. Of course, that affected Leona as well, and it put a great strain on her. Now she is free from all of that, and we will see a much happier Leona.'

'Can't she see events anymore then?' Mollie asked.

'It's become much harder. You can ask her about it if you like. I'm sure she wouldn't mind. Now, breakfast.'

After getting his land rover towed away, Bates reported to his land manager to get the insurance claim sorted out. After that, he considered making a call on Dulap, but what good would it do? Wottle was not a man he could bully; he'd get no joy there. But the boy, Ethan, was a different matter. He would know if his partner-in-arms had damaged his property. In fact, he was probably there when the crime was done. He had to be careful though; losing his temper with Ethan could backfire, and the police would not take kindly to him taking the law into his own hands. But, If he could get the boy on his own, just for a few minutes, he might ask questions in such a way that would intimidate the lad. He knew where the two met up and approximately what time, so, tomorrow, he would try to intercept him.

To Bates's annoyance, he saw no sign of Ethan for the next two days. Probably lying low, laughing at his expense. On the third morning, he spotted Ethan walking slowly to the meeting place. Bates stood in his way.

'Hello. Ethan, going to meet Dulap?'

'What do you want, Mr Bates?'

'Well now, Ethan, I found that my very expensive land rover has been vandalised. Windows broken, paintwork scratched, and the boot forced open. One of my rifles was missing, too. Do you know anything about it?'

'No, I don't. It's the first time I've heard about it. Dulap has said nothing, either. If that's all, I'm going now.'

'Not so fast, lad. I know you're great pals with Dulap. Go about together all the time, don't you?' 'I've seen you on the moors, where you have no right to be, trespassing and interfering with things that don't concern either of you. I remember you used to go there on your own and I'm not so sure that you had nothing to do with my attack. Still, we won't talk about that now. Go on, get on your way, Ethan. I don't want to see you on the moors again. Do you understand me?'

Ethan saw Dulap coming towards them, so he barged by the gamekeeper to meet him. Bates looked at them, then walked away with purpose.

'What did he want?' asked Dulap.

'He wanted to talk to me about his land rover being vandalised. I'm glad you came when you did.'

'Well, never mind about him. We'll just stay away from the moors for a while until things calm down a bit. Come on, let's go for a good, long walk. It's a good day to be outside.'

CHAPTER TWELVE

Christmas day was going to be a joyous occasion at the farm. No one was going to speculate about plans or events until the New Year. For now, they would be all together. Ethan and Mattie had carefully decorated a tree which stood in the living room and another one in front of the kitchen window. The table was laid for six people, which included Jack and Dulap. This would be a special Christmas for him, as he had spent it alone for as long as he could remember, with the inevitable trip to the pub for his festive meal.

Before Dulap arrived, Susan and Jack were preparing the vegetables and whispering. The others were in the living room.

'Peter is recovering well,' Jack was saying, 'however, I think we will need to make some sort of plan. Work will begin on the farm in earnest soon. The cows will calve, and there's lambing too. My honest opinion is that Peter cannot manage this year. As for the future, who knows? We are all going to have a serious talk about the future of the business. What do you think?'

'Yes, you're right, Jack. I was rather hoping that Peter would have recovered enough by now or, at the very least, be doing some jobs around the farm. He just doesn't seem to have the motivation, and we may have to face the fact that he has lost interest. He wasn't born into a farming life; even with your help, he was struggling. Also, how much longer can you neglect your own farm to help us out?'

Jack gave Susan a quick kiss on the cheek and put the potatoes into the roasting tin, ready for the oven. 'Don't worry, Susan, I have been giving the situation a great deal of thought. There are solutions, even if some of them might seem radical. Of course, it all depends on whether Peter wants to keep the farm and what the rest of you think. Anyway, let's have a great Christmas. I'm glad Dulap's coming; he is always good company. I think that might be him now. Ethan's going to answer it. I'll open a bottle of wine.'

Dulap had arrived, wearing a light green suit, complete with a shirt and floral tie. He gave Susan a hug, shook hands with Jack, taking the glass of wine offered to him; then he walked into the living room with Ethan, to greet Mattie and Peter.

'Hello, how's it going? Hey, I love your tree. I've bought a few gifts, so I'll put them with the others under the tree.'

Mattie greeted him. 'Hello, Dulap. We thought we would leave the present opening until after lunch. There's something for you, too.'

'Yes,' joined in Peter, 'it's nice to have you here. After all, you've become part of the family. Do sit down; help yourself to another drink, and there are some nibbles on the table over there.'

'Thank you kindly; I'll do just that. I hear you haven't been well lately. How are you now, Peter? You know, I'm always on hand to help if needed. I've never had a farm myself, only a small holding of sorts, but I have some experience of farming.'

Susan popped her head round the door. 'Anyone for a top-up? Or a beer? What about you, Mattie?'

'I wouldn't mind another glass of orange, Mum. I'll come and get it.'

'No,' answered Susan, 'I'll bring a jug in and the wine bottle as well, so, stay where you are. Lunch will be ready in about an hour, so just relax, all of you. Jack and I have everything under control.'

Mattie settled back with her drink. Her moods had stabilised, and she felt happier than she had been for months. She was content to let the others talk without her input. Ethan sat near, just listening.

'How's life in the woods, Dulap? No trouble with Bates, is there?' Peter asked, 'I know you've had run-ins recently. It's difficult to keep things quiet in a village. Ethan doesn't tell us much.'

'Yes,' answered Dulap, 'best to keep out of his way, but it's not always easy. Did you tell your Dad about your unexpected meeting with him, Ethan?'

'Really, Ethan, is that right? You never mentioned it. What did he say to you?'

Ethan shrugged. 'It wasn't much, really. He asked me if I knew anything about his range rover. Someone had vandalised it; he seemed to think that I might have had something to do with it. As if! I was glad to see Dulap coming along the path to meet me because I could see that Bates wasn't happy about my answers. I mean, what would I know about his stupid car.'

Peter looked from Ethan to Dulap with concern. 'I see. Dulap, did you know Bates accused Ethan of attacking him? I don't like the man either, but someone is out to get him.'

'Bates had no right to question the lad like that,' Dulap answered. 'I admit we spend some time watching him from a safe distance; that's because he's breaking the law, destroying nests and killing birds. Don't worry, I always keep Ethan at a safe distance. I'll not let anything happen to him.'

Peter let it go, although unconvinced by Dulap's reply. Susan called them to the table, and the mood lightened.

Christmas lunch was a great success, with the traditional turkey and Mattie choosing the nut roast, especially made for her, by Jack. Everyone was in a good mood, talking about anything, from the recent snow to Mattie's plans for the garden, with a bit of politics and philosophy thrown in. The Christmas tree brought a wonderful light and festive feel to the day; candles were lit with scents of spices, vanilla and frankincense. Susan brought out a second box of expensive crackers and then lit the pudding, after soaking it with brandy. Afterwards, everyone helped with clearing the table, washing up, drying and putting everything away while Jack made coffee.

Then the presents were opened. Dulap had made little animal figures for them all; each one carefully and skilfully worked and then polished. His new yellow cotton shirt, a colourful addition to his wardrobe, delighted him. Ethan was very pleased with a telescope and tripod, while Mattie opened her gift to discover a new set of paints and an easel. Peter gave Susan a jumper, gloves and scarf in her favourite colour and was a little uncomfortable with the set of earrings from Jack. He received books, and Peter, a new jacket. Dulap stayed until late and was invited back for tea the next day.

In another part of the village, in the vicarage, the Reverend Samuel Canning and his wife, Imogen, sat, eating their meal, but without the same carefree relaxation. They had been married for four years; within that time, Imogen had hoped for a baby. Now, each month, her hopes were unfulfilled, only to bring sadness and hopelessness in its wake. She wanted them to have medical tests just to see if there was a problem, and if so, what they could do about it.

Samuel looked at his wife. He saw yet another disappointment, which showed clearly on her face. Well, this couldn't go on. He had hoped that medical intervention would be unnecessary, but he feared that if he didn't agree to a trip to the doctor, Imogen would become worse. He knew the problem was urgent. She was obsessed with having a baby, and he had to act.

'My dear, I will go to the surgery with you and try to sort this out. I know what this means to you.'

Imogen showed a slight smile and answered, 'Really, Samuel? We need to do this. You really understand, don't you? The entire process could take some time. We might have to see a specialist, and then, well, who knows? I'll make an appointment just as soon as the holidays are over. I feel better already.'

'Good,' replied Samuel, 'that's that, then. By the way, I expected you to be at the service today. It looks bad when my wife doesn't support me. Of course, no one said anything, but I know what they are thinking.'

Imogen bridled. 'Really, Samuel, that's just too bad. Going to church has been difficult for me recently. I can pray on my own, and besides, you can bring communion to me so I'm not missing out. I'll see how I feel after we see the doctor.'

Samuel conceded to his wife's demands. What else could he do? Life without his darling Imogen was unthinkable. He would do whatever he had to do to keep her.

Gamekeeper Bates lived on his own; his wife had left him years ago and taken his son with her. As far as he was concerned, he was well rid of them both. She had never asked for money, and that suited him too. Every Christmas, the Estate Manager invited him to join him and his family. The food was always good; the ten-year-old malt whisky was especially welcome. He enjoyed the day immensely, staying well after midnight as he could walk home. Yes, life was looking up. He had a secure job and home and more than enough money for his means. There was only one problem in his world, and that was in the shape of Dulap Whottle and his sidekick, Ethan. Well, he would sort them out next year. He would stop their interference.

Perhaps the most peaceful and spiritual Christmas was shared by Leona, Mona and Mollie. It was not exactly how Mona had imagined her life to be. She had hoped that Mollie's father would have kept in touch for the sake of her daughter, or maybe she might have met someone else. Mollie had two excellent female role models, but she knew the importance of a good father in her life as well. Still, at least they had found security and a very special friend. For now, pull another cracker and have a second helping of pudding.

CHAPTER THIRTEEN

Early January was cold, with frosty mornings; Peter had joined Jack on the farm again and seemed to have gained much of his enthusiasm for the work. Jack didn't want his friend to have a relapse; besides, he needed to get back to his own farm. Jack had asked Dulap to help, especially over the lambing time.

Susan and Mattie had just finished breakfast when Mattie said, 'I saw you, Mum, with Jack, kissing.'

Susan felt her face redden. 'I knew there was someone on the stairs; I just didn't know who. You need to know that this didn't start when Jack moved in. We have been seeing each other for some time. Also, it's not why I asked him to live here. You must believe me, Mattie.'

'Yes, I do. I'm not judging you, Mum. I know you and Dad don't share a bedroom anymore. Still, it was a shock because I didn't know about this. What will happen? Are you going to leave Dad?'

'I really haven't thought that far ahead. I'm just living from day to day, doing the best I can for everyone. Have you given any more thought to your future, darling?'

'I know what I won't do, Mum, university isn't for me. Some practical courses nearer to home would be the plan or a course online. I'm going to send lots of prospectuses. Anyway, I can't help Dad anymore. I'm not even sure of the ethics of keeping animals.'

Mattie went to her bedroom to look up courses while Susan washed the breakfast things, after which she wandered outside to join

Jack and Peter. She shuddered with the cold. Even with her jumper and warm coat, it seemed to invade her body, and her feet were freezing. Peter had never been what one could call hardy; he was always complaining about the winter weather, the ice and the snow. Susan would never understand why he had become a farmer. She asked if they wanted a flask of coffee.

'No,' Peter replied, 'we'll come in for a bit. We need to talk to you, anyway.'

'Right then, coffee and biscuits will be on the table in a few minutes.'

'There are several alternatives to how the farm can be managed,' Peter began. 'One idea is to sell the cows, concentrate on the sheep and maybe diversify. That would have to be looked into carefully, but it is something that other farms have done successfully. Jack has some good ideas about all this, and he is happy to do some research and look at the finances, too.'

'Yes, I'll be happy to do that,' replied Jack, 'also, we want to ask Dulap if he would be interested in putting in some regular hours on the farm; that would really help Peter. He touched on that at Christmas, I seem to remember.'

'I see,' said Susan, 'I'll go along with whatever you two decide. Mattie certainly can't help at the moment. She is looking into courses that she might start this year. What none of us want is for you to be ill again, Peter. With the calving season and lambing coming up, it's going to be a very busy time.'

'I'll have to be thinking about my sheep,' added Jack, 'I'll go back tomorrow full time. I have a couple of lads who help me.'

Susan tried not to show her disappointment after Jack's announcement. She'd have a word in private later. Right now, there was someone else she needed to catch up with. She hardly saw Ethan these days. He hadn't come down for breakfast, so she knocked on his door.

'Come in.'

'Only me, Ethan, I've brought you tea.'

'Thanks, Mum. Is everything ok?'

'Sure, I just thought it would be nice to have a catch-up with my son.'

'Fine. I saw Dad and Jack in the yard. They seemed to be deep in conversation.'

Susan nodded. 'Things are going through a few changes. Your father doesn't want the farm to stay the same. He's thinking of selling the cows but keeping the sheep. There'll be a lot of planning and research to do; Jack can help with that. What about you, Ethan? Are you happy? Doing what you want to do? Can I help you with anything?'

Ethan sipped his tea. 'The answer to that question is partly. I really enjoy my time with Dulap. He's taught me so much, but I realise I also have to move on with my life too. Don't misunderstand me, Mum. Nothing will ever take the place of my work and studies with Dulap. I'd like to study ornithology but mainly work on my own or with him.'

'Your dad is going to ask Dulap if he wants to help him on the farm?'

This news clearly annoyed Ethan. He slammed the cup on the bedside table. 'Why can't he manage on his own or get some farm hand to help? What about Jack?'

'Jack helps all he can, but he needs to get back to his own farm now. Dulap won't work full time, but it will be regular hours, especially during lambing. He could do with the money, too.'

'Dulap and I have important things we have to do as well. Nothing must interfere with that.'

'Yes, I understand, Ethan. Is there anything you want to talk to me about?'

'No, there isn't,' Ethan said sharply. 'Is Mattie around?'

'She's in her bedroom, looking at courses online. It would be nice for you two to talk more. Anyway, I'm glad we had a chat. I'll see you downstairs then.'

Susan glanced around the room before she left. Everything was so neat, so ordered; the bed made perfectly. Books stacked in neat piles, furniture polished and clothes ironed and folded neatly. Ethan had always been the same from an early age. He was a loner and made few friends at school. His homework had always been completed early every evening; its presentation neat and well-written. Because of his self-isolation, he was unpopular with his peers and was glad to leave school. Then came a period of semi-seclusion, even from Susan. Meeting Dulap had been an unexpected but life-changing event for Ethan. He didn't want to share his newfound friend to work on the farm. Despite this, a few days later, Dulap arrived to discuss work with Peter.

'Ethan is critical about the state of my cottage. He's quite right, too. It's badly in need of repair and redecoration.' He winked at Ethan. 'I didn't realise just what a dump my home was becoming. The holding pens could do with improving, as well as tidying the garden.'

Ethan looked on but said nothing. It was all arranged, with Dulap starting with the commencement of lambing. At first, that would mean all day. Ethan slipped away, going to his bedroom, not even responding when Susan called up to him that Dulap was going.

She knocked on his door later.

'Ethan, what's the matter? Let me in, please.'

The door opened slightly. Susan could see he'd been crying.

'I suppose you and Dad are pleased with yourselves? If he can't manage the farm, he shouldn't have taken it on. We all knew it was a mistake. Why is he taking Dulap from me?'

'It's only for a few months or whenever your Dad needs extra help. I'm sure Dulap needs the money as well, especially if he wants to improve his cottage; he said something about repairs and decoration. Why are you so upset, Ethan? Your dad won't stand between you and Dulap.'

85

'I don't expect you to understand,' Ethan retorted, 'Dulap is the only real, genuine friend I have ever had. I introduced him to my family, and now other people want a piece of him. What about my plans, Mum? You don't know the important work we are undertaking. You just don't get it. Of course, Dulap agreed to help Dad, because he's a nice man and could see what a mess Dad had got himself in. Why can't Mattie help like she used to? Oh, just go away! Leave me alone.' With that, Ethan slammed the door in Susan's face and locked it.

'Please talk to me, Ethan. I want to help you and understand how you are feeling. Don't shut me out. I'm on your side; I always have been.'

'I said, go away.'

Susan joined Mattie in the living room.

'What was all that shouting about?' Mattie asked.

'Ethan's a bit upset. He didn't want to talk to me, so I'll just have to wait until he does. I have some understanding of how he's feeling. Sometimes, we all forget how sensitive he is. Remember what a tough time he had at school? I was relieved when he left that place at last. He never made friends and was bullied, if only verbally.'

'Yes, Mum, I know about all those times you went to see the Head and when you kept him at home. There were one or two teachers who were sympathetic, but nothing changed much. Shall I try to talk to him? We used to be so close. He might open up to me.'

'That would be wonderful, Mattie; wait a while until he's calmed down and then attempt to talk. Perhaps not today, though. I get the impression that he would like to discuss things with you, as well.'

'I'll talk to him, Mum, don't worry.'

Ethan stayed upstairs for about an hour, then came downstairs, made a sandwich and a flask of coffee, and went out. Susan and Mattie let him go without another word.

CHAPTER FOURTEEN

February brought a genuine change in the weather despite more frosty mornings and chill east winds. Since her extraordinary vision, Leona had not wanted to leave the house, so, today, she was spending time in the garden. She was delighted to see frogs in the pond, knowing that spawn would follow. She might even get a glimpse of the great-crested newts later on when the sun would bring them to the top of the water. Leona had avoided putting fish into the pond; she wasn't overfond of golden carp, which would eat the young amphibians.

It was time for the rooks to repair their ravished nests, spending more time sitting on them and going short distances to forage for food. Blackbirds attacked the pyracantha berries, and a male sparrowhawk, with his slate-blue back, swept down silently, causing general panic within the wild bird population.

Mollie knew something had happened to Leona but didn't know what that was. Mona had suggested that she ought to ask Leona herself. Mollie said that she would.

'Good,' Mona said, 'I need to go to the post office anyway and thought I would treat myself to coffee and cake, so that will give you plenty of time to have your talk.'

Mollie joined Leona in the garden. 'Well, Mollie, everything is looking fine, just some weeding and tying-up to do. I'm looking forward to sitting out here again.'

'You're much happier now, aren't you, Leona?'

'I'm very happy now, Mollie. How about you?'

'Much happier here. I didn't used to be when I lived in the other house though.'

Leona frowned. 'Why was that, Mollie?'

'Well, I loved my Dad until he quarrelled with Mum. She cried a lot, and I didn't know how to help her. I miss him, and I'd like to see him again, now I'm living with you and Mum. Can I ask you something, Leona?'

'Of course, come and sit over here on the bench. It's fairly dry. You can always talk to me. How can I help?'

'Mum said something happened to you after your walk. When you came back, you were happy and smiling. I've never seen you like that before. Mum said I should ask you about it.'

'Oh, I see. Well, I don't mind telling you, although I can't explain what happened fully. When I went out, I had no plans to walk to a particular place or the way I should go. I just wandered about, usually taking the public rights of way. One of these suddenly led into a large wood. It was strange because I hadn't noticed the trees before me. Anyway, I hadn't walked far but was feeling tired, so I found a fallen log to sit on. It had been silent, but suddenly, the air was filled with the most beautiful bird song. It may sound fanciful, Mollie, but the wood seemed to welcome me. I suppose I had been sitting for a few minutes when I saw figures approaching me. I couldn't see them clearly; they were so bright, and it hurt my eyes. Then, I saw someone with them, and my mother stood in front of me. There was no doubt about who it was.'

'That's strange,' Mollie said, 'is your Mum still alive then?'

'No, she died some time ago. I wasn't frightened, why would I be? I had no fear of her when she was alive. The vision did fade then, but all my fears and doubts left me. I had one more experience, though. There was a man there, too, and when he vanished, I felt a peace which is difficult to describe. It has faded somewhat now, but I shall never forget its effect on me.'

Mollie thought for a while, then asked, 'Can you take me to this wood? I would love to go.'

'Maybe, Mollie, but I have a feeling that this place doesn't always want to be found. I think your Mum will be back soon. Will you help me with the washing-up?'

When Mona came home, she unpacked the shopping and gave a bunch of tulips to Leona. 'Can you find a vase for these, Mollie? There should be one under the sink. What have you two been up to while I've been away?' Leona winked at Mona, saying, 'Mollie and I have been chatting. She wanted to know about my experience, and I told her the whole story.'

'Really. What do you think about that, Mollie?'

'Oh, Mum, it was so nice. I wish something like that would happen to me. If I found the wood, it might.'

'Well,' answered Mona, 'if it's meant to happen, then it will.'

The doorbell rang; Mollie answered it. 'Mum, it's Dad.'

Malcolm entered the kitchen, clearly embarrassed. 'Sorry to come round unannounced. Can we talk?'

'We haven't seen you since we left. Why now? Oh, this is my friend, Leona.'

'Yes,' Malcolm answered, 'I didn't have your address at first, and when you wrote to tell me where you were, I didn't know whether to come round. Of course, I wanted to see Mollie very much. I shouldn't have let so much time go by. Still, I'm here now.'

Mollie wasn't sure what to do, so she stood by Mona. Leona went into the living room to wait.

'So,' continued Mona, 'you say you want to see Mollie? If you're really serious about this and providing Mollie wants this, we can come to some arrangement. What do you think, darling?'

'I would like to see Dad if that's o.k. with you, Mum?'

'Of course it is. I'm happy about it if you are. So, what about every other weekend and day during the school holidays? We can always change it as circumstances dictate.'

After Malcolm had gone and Mollie was in bed, Mona confided in Leona. 'It was quite a shock to see Malcolm. He certainly took his time to come forward. As far as Mollie is concerned, I think she thought he had abandoned her. Now, he gives a pathetic apology and says he wants to see her. Still, I'm glad he came, for Mollie's sake.'

'Was he a good father when you lived together?'

'Yes, he was. I suppose he could have shown more interest in Mollie's schoolwork and her interests, but he was always loving towards her. It will be good for her to have her father in her life again.

By the way, did she react well when you told her you had seen your mother?'

'She did. I thought she might be frightened; after all, I was telling her I had seen a dead person. It didn't bother her, just interested.' Leona laughed. 'She wants to visit the woods, but I don't know where it is or how I got there.'

'That's really weird, Leona. How do you feel about everything now? You have had some really major changes lately.'

'Changes that are welcome. I don't miss my work or think it made any serious difference to people's lives. Just tried to help them, and if I did, then I'm happy about that. I have a new life and a fresh start, and I mean to make something of it. Of course, you and Mollie are a large part of that. I realise you may not always live here, and I accept that, but we will always be the best of friends.'

'The three of us will always be close,' answered Mona, 'whatever happens.'

CHAPTER FIFTEEN

Imogen and Samuel were having breakfast. The day was chilly for early March, with late frosts and brief snow showers. He was ready for his meeting with the Church committee. Imogen was eating in her nightclothes. Although the room was warm, she wrapped her dressing gown tightly around herself for a feeling of comfort and security, her dark shoulder-length hair drawn back in a ponytail.

Samuel would leave for work soon, so she had all morning to herself, which pleased her. He poured another coffee; he had something to say to Imogen, which he knew wouldn't please her.

'The Committee has asked if you would help with the monthly "Big Breakfast" event. They also need help with arranging the flowers in the church, as Mrs Spencer isn't well. Also, Easter will be here soon, and you know how busy that is.'

Imogen buttered another slice of toast, ate half and met her husband's gaze.

'Really, Samuel, you know how difficult I'm finding everything just now. Sorry, I really can't help with all these things at the moment. I'm sure the committee will manage somehow.'

'Are you depressed, Imogen? Is this about having a baby?'

'Of course it is, Samuel. I realise you don't give the same importance to this as I do, but surely you understand the way I feel. What's more important, the committee's wishes or your wife's?'

Samuel felt exasperated. Not this again. Life didn't stop because Imogen wasn't pregnant.

'I'm doing all I can to support you, Imogen. We've both had all the tests and the doctors have assured us that there is no obstacle to us having a baby. However, this will not happen unless there is a certain amount of intimacy between us. Those occasions have been few lately.'

Imogen tried to stay calm, and she knew there was truth in what Samuel had said.

'Well, I want to concentrate on the two days each month when I can conceive, which is why I take my temperature every day, so I know when there's a slight rise, which means I'm ovulating. I have explained this to you before.'

'All I can say is,' replied Samuel, 'if we had a normal sex life and you just tried to relax, involving yourself in everyday life, I'm sure you would conceive. Worrying about it all the time is probably preventing the very thing you want to happen.'

Imogen turned her face away, looking out of the window. The snow had stopped. She answered, 'I think I'll get dressed and have a stroll in the garden. I need to order some summer plants as well. You go to your committee meeting, Samuel. I'll see you later.'

Samuel gathered his papers together and rushed out of the room. There was little point in trying to converse with Imogen when she was in this mood.

Not bothering to dress, Imogen put on a coat and rubber boots and going into the large Vicarage garden. She inspected the pots on the patio; the lovely blue and purple iris was nearly finished, but the tulips were developing nicely, promising the usual annual display. The bluebells which she had planted in a large barrel container were doing well too. She swept the fallen leaves from the paving and started on her rounds around the garden, beginning with the roses in the borders. They needed pruning; she fetched the secateurs from the greenhouse. The early red shoots had grown, but to Imogen's surprise, aphids were all over the fresh growth. She rarely sprayed until April, but it certainly needed doing now.

She was feeling cold now. There was nothing else to do in the garden, so she went in. The dishes needed washing, but they could wait. She had all morning to see to them. So, making a fresh coffee, she settled into the big chair in the living room, a cosy throw over her legs, and a book.

After a while of reading, she felt tired and closed her eyes. She was soon asleep, but when she woke, all her sadness had come back. The book and throw had fallen onto the carpet. Imogen got up and looked out of the window. The slight snow had stopped. She needed to get out, away from the stifling atmosphere of the vicarage. It was cold, but if she wore her big coat, gloves and boots, she would be fine. Outside was still and calm. Turning left, out of the vicarage gates, Imogen kept to the road for a while, but, like Mona before her, she found herself on the path leading to the cottage in the clearing.

Before she could turn back, Dulap came out. 'No, don't go, lass. You've come here for a reason, even if you don't know what that is yet. You look cold; come in and sit by the fire. There's always a pot of coffee on the stove.'

Imogen was startled. What a strange man. Who on earth was he? She did, however, have a vague recollection of hearing about a man like this with a strange name.

'Are you called Dulap?'

'I am, lass. You've no need to fear me. Will you come in and get warm?'

Imogen sat near the open fire. The blaze warmed her; she felt relaxed and welcomed here. While Dulap poured the coffee, she took in her surroundings. Maybe it needed some small repairs and a touch of paint, but it was clean and so homely.

'Are you married to the Minister?' Dulap asked.

'Yes, I am. How did you know? You don't go to church, do you?' Imogen laughed. 'Mind you, I haven't been for weeks; me, the vicar's wife. I can't face going at the moment. Oh, I'm sorry, I really don't know why I'm telling you all this. I'll drink my coffee and get on my way home.'

'Hey, it's fine, lass. You need to unburden yourself. I'm a good listener, and anything you tell me will go no further.'

Imogen hesitated. Why did she want to talk about her troubles with a stranger? Still, she needed someone to talk to, and he was here now.

Dulap looked hard at her. 'Am I right in saying you don't have children?'

'No, I don't, and it colours my whole life and causes me great sadness. I'm in my mid-thirties and the desire for a baby is strong in me. I try to talk to Samuel about how I feel, but, as that's all I talk about, he's understandably fed up with listening. And then... oh, it doesn't matter.'

'I'm sorry to hear about your troubles. I've never fathered children; well, not that I know of, anyway. Are there medical reasons to explain why you're not conceiving?'

Imogen sighed. 'Not really. Samuel and I have had all the tests and medical procedures available. We are both healthy. The trouble is, it's become like a military operation, keeping a record of my monthly cycle; that's all my diary is full of. I know I should support Samuel. After all, I knew that would be an important role for me before I married him. But getting involved with church matters is such a chore, and he has become very reproachful. I can see it in his eyes. The only time I go to church these days is when it's empty.'

'I'm sure things will sort themselves out,' Dulap answered, 'there's still plenty of time for a baby. Now, I'll tell you what I'm going to do. I'm going to be busy soon, helping with lambing. I can't say for sure when I will be at home, so, I'm going to give you a key to the cottage. Then, if you want somewhere to get away for a while, you can let yourself in any time you want.'

'Are you sure about this, Dulap?'

'Yes, absolutely. Just make sure that you lock up before you leave. Here you are; I always keep a spare set.'

Imogen put the key in her coat pocket. 'Thank you, Dulap, I'll keep it safe. I'd better go now. I'm feeling a lot better. Maybe you've given me some hope. Bye, Dulap and thank you.'

When Imogen returned home, her first job was to tackle the washing-up. Samuel would be home soon; she didn't want him to know that she'd been out. What had she been thinking of, telling a stranger all her personal problems? What if she couldn't trust him and the entire village learnt about her intimate life? Samuel would never forgive her; their marriage might not recover from such disclosures. It had been so easy to talk to that kind, strange man. Looking back, it was as though Dulap had been waiting for her to visit him. Of course, that was ridiculous...

Imogen had just finished putting the dishes away when Samuel walked in.

'Well, that was a very successful parish meeting. We got a lot done; in fact, everything I wanted to discuss. How have you been, my love? You look a lot brighter than you did at breakfast.'

'Yes, I do. I read for a bit and walked in the garden. How about some sandwiches for lunch? I'm sure you could do with something to eat.'

Samuel smiled. The change in Imogen encouraged him, and he hoped it would last. 'Yes, lovely. I'll be in the study, sorting out my notes in some sort of order.'

'Maybe I could help you with that, Samuel? I can type the minutes for you. I know I have been little help lately, but do call on my help if you need me. Only, I'm not quite up to meeting people yet.'

'Yes, if you could type up the minutes, it would be a great help.' It delighted Samuel that his wife was showing an interest in church affairs again. It was a start, anyway. True, she wasn't ready to take on her other duties, but that was sure to change soon.

Husband and wife spent a pleasant evening together, discussing parish business and Imogen's plans for the summer garden. Before Imogen went to bed, she retrieved the key from her coat pocket, putting it safely on her key ring. She thought about the little cottage and its occupant. Yes, she would pay another visit to the clearing in the woods soon. That thought made her happy.

CHAPTER SIXTEEN

Jack wanted Susan to move in. He needed to persuade her, but how? Moor Farm was her home; he doubted she would ever leave, especially as Mattie and Ethan needed her; both were floundering; neither had a clue how to move forward. Mattie had loved working on the farm; now she didn't. As for Ethan, his only companion was a man old enough to be his grandfather. So, for the time being, he would have to be content with Susan's visits until things changed. It encouraged him that Mattie knew about their relationship, and she hadn't made a fuss or told Peter.

All was peaceful at the Vicarage; Samuel was convinced his wife was happy; Imogen had even attended church services again, although not every week. She hadn't talked about babies for weeks.

He was visiting the church when he saw Mrs Peters walking towards him and waving. Another of his "ladies", who kept his church clean and the pews and lecterns dust-free and shiny. However, this woman made it her duty to gossip about the lives of all who lived in the village, and she was rarely wrong.

'Hello, Mrs Peters. How are you today? I'm on my way to the church. It's looking its best.'

She stood in front of him, looking embarrassed. 'Oh yes, vicar, everything is in order there, but I'm afraid I've heard about something which I feel you should know.'

'Now, Mrs Peters, I'm sure whatever it is can't be all that bad. You know I don't like to gossip.'

'I have seen...oh dear, this is so awkward, but it concerns your wife.'

Samuel became defensive and annoyed, but he needed to know what this woman knew about Imogen.

'I'm sure I can't imagine what you mean, Mrs Peters. Whatever it is, you had better tell me. Let's go to the church. It's not a good idea to be talking on the road.'

Five minutes later, they were sitting in the vestry.

'Now, Mrs Peters, out with it, please.'

'Well, I have seen your wife frequently, coming and going along a path which leads to the cottage of a certain individual. I fear she has been visiting there for several months. Of course, I wanted to say something earlier, but I needed to be sure of my facts. Forgive me, vicar, but I actually followed her one day, and there she was, sitting outside, drinking tea. She didn't see me, I was very careful.'

'And was my wife on her own?'

'Oh, yes, she was. But don't you think it's odd? People don't normally sit outside someone else's property unless they know the person.'

Samuel bridled. 'I don't want to hear another word about this. Do you understand, Mrs Peters? Talking about my wife in this way, it will be all perfectly innocent. There can be no doubt about that. Whatever concerns you have, my dear Imogen has done nothing wrong. And now, if you don't mind, I have matters to attend to, so good morning.'

The woman hurried away in tears, leaving Samuel worried. What did this all mean? Imogen, going to see some man; sneaking off without a word to him. Something strange was going on that he knew nothing about. He felt embarrassed. Well, he was going home to confront Imogen.

Arriving back, he found Imogen resting on her favourite chair, with the high back and leg rest.

'Samuel, I'm so glad you're home early. I have some wonderful news.'

'Really, Imogen? I have something important to ask you first.'

'Why are you talking like this? You seem to have returned in a foul mood. Well, it won't dampen my happiness.'

Samuel sat on the sofa, facing his wife. 'I've been talking to Mrs Peters. You know, the woman who polishers and cleans the church.'

Imogen laughed. 'Oh well, now I know why you've come back in such a bad mood.'

Samuel replied, 'I was subject to a rather puzzling conversation with her. She told me you are in the habit of visiting a man and sitting outside his cottage.'

'Don't be so dramatic, Samuel. I admit I have been there a few times, but usually, I am by myself. If I want a hot drink, I can go inside and make it,'

'You have access to this cottage then?'

'Well, yes, I do; I have a key. I like to be there on my own. There's no harm in it.'

'But, my dear,' Samuel answered, 'you have a lovely home here and a delightful garden, which you have lavished attention on and spent a lot of my money, I may add.'

Imogen sighed. 'Sometimes, I just want to get away from the vicarage. Dulap lives in a little cottage in the middle of a woodland clearing. I love going there; it makes me feel like myself again.'

'Dulap, that's his name, is it? Is he as strange as his name?'

'Stop it, Samuel. He's a friend, a kind man, who listened to me when I needed to talk, and you wouldn't listen. I'm not talking about this right now. I'm going to lie down.'

'So, what's this wonderful news you want to tell me, Imogen?'

'Later, not now.'

Samuel knew what Imogen was going to tell him; she was pregnant. Good news indeed, but how could he be sure that the baby was his? He needed to know the truth about her friendship with this man. He must be sure.

Later, Imogen joined him downstairs.

'I have good news to tell you, but you've spoiled it. I'm pregnant, Samuel. Sorry, you're not as delighted as I am.'

'Is it mine, Imogen?'

'Of course; how could you say such a thing?'

'I'm sorry, my dear, but I can't be sure. How long have you been seeing this man?' What exactly is the nature of your relationship?'

'Please don't make an issue of this. I met him quite by chance on one of my walks. He is just a friend, nothing more. If I'd told you, you would have made a fuss.'

Samuel tried to keep his temper under control.

'What did you talk about, Imogen? No, let me guess: your obsession about wanting a baby. I suppose he is now privy to all our personal problems.'

'I didn't mean to tell him about it, but he was so easy to talk to and seeing him really helped me. Please try to understand, Samuel.'

Samuel didn't understand. He retired to his study; he had to think. Why had she done this to him? He slept in the spare room and went out early in the morning. Imogen was unhappy now, but he couldn't speak to her. Deciding to see this Dulap and make sense of this situation, and above all, to find out if this baby was this man's or his, he needed to find out where he lived. The best course of action was to go to "The Lapwing". Surely someone would know him there.

The pub had just opened when Samuel walked in. Not too busy yet, good.

'What can I get for you, sir?'

'Half a lager, please. Do you know a man called Dulap?'

The landlord laughed. 'Old Dulap, yes, he's in here most days. Sit down. He'll probably be in soon. I'll let him know you want to speak to him.'

Dulap came in ten minutes later, glanced at Samuel and went to the bar. He sat down with him.

'Dulap's the name. You want to see me? What can I do for you? No job too small.'

The vicar felt an uncontrollable jealousy. There was something about this man that he liked instinctively, and that was the last thing he wanted to feel. He was a little strangely dressed, and Samuel thought the ponytail ridiculous, but the face had an open honesty and friendliness. Dulap was popular with everyone who came in; some offered to buy him another drink.

Samuel steadied himself and asked, 'Is it true that you have been seeing my wife, Imogen? She didn't tell me; I found out another way, but she has admitted it. Do you think it proper to invite another man's wife into your home?'

'Imogen came by my place by accident,' replied Dulap. 'She was cold and in some distress, so I wanted to help her. I sat her by the fire, gave her a coffee, and listened. Nothing she told me has gone any further. I'm sorry you're upset; I understand, but I meant no harm.'

'I see. My wife informed me she is pregnant. Can you appreciate my concern? I need your reassurance that I am the father of this baby.'

Dulap smiled. 'I can't think why you would think otherwise, vicar. You're very blessed. Nice meeting you; I need another drink after this.'

It did not satisfy Samuel; his doubts persisted. He walked home. Imogen was in her favourite chair, with a blanket around her. She heard him come in but looked away, not wanting to talk. Samuel stood in the doorway and said, 'I saw that man, Dulap. I can see why you're attracted to him, my dear; he is somewhat on the elderly side, but he has a lot of charm. Unfortunately, although I spoke to him about you, he could not satisfy the only question I want answering. I'll be in the study.'

Imogen closed her eyes, leaning back into the soft comfort of the armchair. She would swear the baby was Samuel's, but she knew it wasn't.

CHAPTER SEVENTEEN

Who was that? Too tall to be the boy, and wasn't Dulap's style. He usually kept his distance, but he rarely hid; this man wanted the gamekeepers to notice him. Bates hoped it wasn't someone new; he was irritated but not unduly worried. No point in trying to apprehend the intruder; he'd be gone before he could walk halfway to him. The police had questioned Bates after they had received photographs of two eggs in the boot of his land rover, and had informed him they were those of a peregrine falcon. Of course, he denied all knowledge of them; they must have been planted there at the time of the vandalism.

Shortly after this, Bates had a message to report to the Estate Manager, Hugh Curtis, a friend and one of the few people who liked the gamekeeper.

'Come in, Bates, fancy a whiskey? I have a good bottle of single malt. Sit yourself down; try this. Now, what's all this about some eggs? Know anything about it?'

'Absolutely not, boss. Can't help you there. You're right; this is a wonderful whiskey.

'I'm not accusing you of any wrongdoing. I know you cut a few corners in your work, and that's fine as long as the law doesn't get involved. The owners are worried about adverse publicity. You do a good job; just be careful.'

'Of course,' replied Bates. 'Someone tried to set me up, planting those eggs in the boot.'

'I believe you. I talked to the owners, and they seemed satisfied. Top up?'

'Please,' said Bates, 'by the way, I've seen a stranger walking the moors. I don't think it's that bastard, Dulap. I'll keep my eye on the situation.'

'Well, just keep me up to date.'

All was well, or so Bates thought. The next day he saw the figure again, and Bates knew he could not tolerate this long term. The other keepers were told to report any sightings. He paid Dulap a visit in case he knew anything about it.

'Well, this is a surprise, Bates, but I guess this isn't a social visit. Come in; say, would you have to?'

'No, I'll talk outside because it won't take long. If you are the mysterious man in black, I'm here to tell you it won't work, Whottle. Is it you?'

Dulap smiled. 'Well now, it could well be me, I really can't say. You'll just have to find out. Seems your troubles never end, do they? Still, all you have to do is change your ways. Stop killing raptors, which have every right to live and breed on the moors.'

Bates scoffed. 'You don't think I'd admit to anything illegal, and you don't really have any proof otherwise, do you? Just some photos of eggs, supposedly taken from the back of my land rover. Really, Whottle, you will have to do better than that. By the way, you know about the rumours circulating about you and the lovely vicar's wife?

Seems like you've been a naughty boy, although what she sees in you, I can't imagine.'

Dulap wanted to hit Bates. He cared little for his own reputation, but he had never meant to hurt Imogen or Samuel. Life for them was going to be tough, especially when her pregnancy showed.

'Malicious talk, Bates, I didn't think even you could be such a bastard. There's no truth to it, anyway.'

'No, of course not,' answered Bates, sarcastically. 'You can't stop the gossip; it's about as exciting as this village gets. I'm going; just remember that I'll be watching you.'

Samuel sat brooding. For days, he had been thinking about the situation he was in. Should he make an appointment to see the Bishop? Ask for a transfer? He would have to explain why and tell him the whole sorry story. What could he do? Imogen didn't acknowledge or care about his concerns. Didn't she see the seriousness of all this? Well, he would have to face the entire village and refute the stories circulating about his marriage.

Imogen popped her head round the door. 'Do you want a coffee, Samuel? I'm trying a new kind; much smoother. Biscuit?'

'Whatever you think, Imogen. I don't mind.'

She was so happy; he had never seen her like this before. Whatever his doubts, how could he spoil it for her now?

Mrs Rogers sat in the tearooms with her best friend, Mrs Gardner, talking about the present topic of interest. Keeping her voice as low as possible, she asked, 'Is there much gossip about the poor vicar and his wife?'

'I'm afraid there is. Do you think there is any truth in it? Are you sure Imogen is pregnant?'

Mrs Rogers nodded. 'I think so, my dear. Believe me, I didn't start the rumours. I wouldn't do such a thing. But I had the unfortunate task of informing the vicar of Imogen's visits to you know who.'

Mrs Gardner shook her head, finishing her scone. 'You say you saw her walking toward his cottage?'

'Oh yes, there was no mistake; that lane only leads there. It's possible that the first time, she simply took the wrong turning, but there were plenty of other times after that. I saw them together, too, when he walked her home. Of course, it could be innocent, but what respectable woman would have anything to do with that old reprobate?'

Mrs Gardner agreed. 'It's the minister I feel sorry for. Such a nice man, too. What did he say when you told him?'

Mrs Rogers sighed. 'Well, he did his best to conceal his surprise, and the defence of his wife was touching, but I could see that he didn't know of the relationship. In fact, he became quite angry towards me. Fancy that, after I had tried to help him. Still, we have a duty to support the head of our church, and he will not find us wanting.'

The women went their separate ways. Mrs Rogers met Dulap on her way home.

'You should be ashamed of yourself, carrying on with another man's wife. The vicar must be heartbroken and such a nice man.'

'You should mind your own business, you old gossip. Get out of my way.'

'Well, really,' Mrs Rogers replied, 'what an awful man you are.' She hurried away.

Dulap arrived at Moor Farm, and Ethan was expecting him.

'Hey, Ethan, are you on your own? Where is everyone?'

'Dad's somewhere on the farm. He's sold the cows; it was Jack's idea. It will make things easier for him. Mum's around somewhere, and Mattie's upstairs studying. She's taking an online course on horticulture. Seems to enjoy it.'

'That all sounds good, Ethan. Let's have a coffee; I could do with a cup. Bates came to the cottage yesterday.'

'What! Why Dulap?'

'He says he's seen someone on the moor. He thinks it might be me, dressed in black and wearing a hood. Bates just doesn't know for sure, and I was noncommittal on the subject. Anyway, it's breeding season, so we have plans to make. There is at least one pair of hen harriers nesting in the heather. They need round-the-clock protection, so, with the help of the local bird society, that's what they will get. I intend to camp just inside the woods; I know where the nest is, and I can monitor it with binoculars. It's the only way to ensure the survival of the parents and their chicks.'

'What can I do?'

'You can keep me supplied with food and hot drinks, please, Ethan. Come to the cottage now and help me get my camping equipment together.'

They watched the quick, soaring flight of the female as she returned to the nest with heather stems, making a platform from the material. If Dulap and Ethan saw her, then so could the gamekeepers. In the evening, as it was getting dark, Dulap set up his tent. He doubted anyone would find him, and the woods didn't belong to the owners of the moors. Ethan joined him during the day, which allowed Dulap to have a quick visit to the cottage when he needed to. Ethan was to observe, make notes, and call the police in case of trouble.

Harriers were seen regularly, flying back and forth to the nest. To Dulap's relief, the birds were being left alone; they must be raising young. He had been prepared to confront Bates head-on if need be, whatever the consequences, but he had rarely seen him. Maybe the gamekeeper knew he was camping near or had been told to leave the birds alone. He thought about Imogen, wondering how she was. He was the father of her baby. She had brought light into his life, and he missed her visits. Oh well, there was nothing he could do about it for the time being.

CHAPTER EIGHTEEN

The visits of Mollie to see Malcolm were going well. She talked about where she had been and what they had done. Mona was glad for her; it also gave her more time for herself. She wanted to expand her life, find interests, and spend time out of the house. At first, a couple of night classes were enough. They were interesting but dull in terms of meeting the right people. What about the possibility of dating? She talked to Leona about it.

'It would be nice to be part of a couple again. My chief concern is Mollie; of course, I'm not talking about getting married, just some male company, that's all. What do you think?'

'You were bound to feel the need for a relationship. After all, you have been on your own for some time. My advice, be careful.'

'I was thinking of online dating. There are success stories about meeting people this way. I'm not looking for anything long-term; I don't feel ready for that, and I'm so happy living here with you and Mollie. I will give it a go.'

'Well,' replied Leona, 'I'm always here to babysit.'

Mona would have preferred to meet men naturally, but how could she do that? Nightclubs were out of the question, and she doubted finding suitable partners at the village pub. Don't rush into anything, and when meetings are arranged, meet during the day to start with.

Relations were better with Malcolm now. Sometimes, when Mollie stayed with him, the three would have a day out. This led to a genuine friendship between them. Now, relaxed in each other's company, the pair talked in a way they had never done when they lived together. Mollie was happy, too, although she secretly hoped they would be a proper family again soon.

The marriage of Imogen and Samuel was in trouble, and, as the months went by and the baby's birth became imminent, the couple felt isolated from each other. He was dreading the event and could not accept that the baby was his. An interview with the bishop was arranged; maybe if he got his wife away from this village, they could make their marriage work again. Imogen was told of the plans.

'I think it advisable to move away; make a fresh start, my dear. So, I have made an appointment with the bishop to discuss the matter. Once the baby is born, speculation will be rife, and my position compromised.'

Imogen looked at Samuel in disbelief.

'I don't want to leave; I like it here. You can't make me leave.'

The vicar looked at the frail, defiant woman before him. He would not tolerate nonsense; if he moved, she would too.

'You have made my ministry untenable, Imogen. I can't think why you made a friend of that man, nor have you been honest with me about that relationship and about the baby. You can't stay here on your own, and we don't own the house, so where would you live? There are no relations in the area either. I suppose it's possible for you to move to Ireland and live with your mother, but both of us will have to leave the vicarage. In the meantime, I suggest you look after yourself and prepare for the birth. Your appetite is not what it should be.'

At that moment, Imogen hated Samuel. He didn't want to be a father to her child, and her own feelings for him were not as they had been. He was right about one thing: her health and that of her baby must be the priority. She made an omelette and felt better for eating it. Then she went upstairs to rest. As she fell asleep, she thought about the peace and security of Dulap's cottage.

Imogen woke suddenly and found her husband bending over her. Startled, she sat up.

'What are you doing, Samuel? It's unpleasant to find you so close to my face. Is something the matter?'

Samuel sat on the bed.

'No, I was just admiring your lovely face. You looked so beautiful lying there. Can I get you anything?'

'I see. Please, don't do that again. I'll be down soon. A cup of tea would be nice.'

As she made her way downstairs, she felt the baby moving. Not long to go now. What happens then, who knows?

'You will let me know the bishop's decision as soon as you hear? This affects me, too. I have my own plans to make.'

Samuel took no notice of Imogen's outbursts. She had no money of her own; her threats were meaningless. Living on her own! What a ridiculous notion. It satisfied him that all would go his way. However, although the bishop listened to the regrettable troubles within the marriage and was sympathetic. He could only promise to consider Samuel's request and reassured him that if a living became vacant, it might be possible for the couple to move. He could not give a timescale.

It was obvious to Imogen that the meeting had not gone as well as Samuel as hoped. She felt a great relief and asked, 'What did the bishop say to your request?'

Samuel busied himself with some papers, answering, 'Oh, it went very well. He will help me and feels sure that another position will become available soon.'

'But not immediately?'

'No, not immediately, as you say, my dear.'

As Samuel walked away, Imogen felt a sudden sadness and regret that they had reduced their marriage to a few occasional conversations, making neither of them happy.

Towards the end of summer, a baby girl was born. It had been a long labour and a difficult birth, but she was healthy and a good weight and took well to breastfeeding. These were days of happiness and contentment for the mother, completely lost in her own world. Samuel did his best to express an interest in the baby, but he felt conflicting emotions, not knowing how to act. Out of his depth, he left them alone.

Imogen wanted Dulap to know about the baby. A week later, she made her way to the cottage, hoping he was at home.

'Well, come in, lass' it's good to see you and the baby. I knew the birth must be soon. Boy or girl?'

'A girl. She's awake. Would you like to hold her? Just support the head. I haven't decided on a name yet. Of course, I'll have to record the birth. I'm not sure who to name as the father?'

'I assume you will name Samuel; I don't know what else you can do. You are married to him, after all. Think about it, lass.'

Imogen took the baby back to feed her.

'I know you are her father, Dulap, and whether I stay with Samuel won't alter that fact. She laughed, and said, 'I don't think giving her the name of Whottle would do her a kindness. The only other option is to give her my maiden name. Samuel doesn't love her; he's had little to do with either of us since the birth.'

' He may, lass, he may give him a chance. She is beautiful, like you.'

Imogen smiled at him. 'Can I come again, Dulap? I'd like to. You cheer me up.'

'Of course you can. Come anytime you like. I'll never turn you away. Have you still got the key?'

'Yes, it's in my purse. Samuel knows I have it, but he hasn't mentioned it recently. I don't suppose he'd think I'd see you. Oh, Dulap, why is life so complicated? I thought in my innocence that when I got married, I would always be happy with Samuel, but I'm not.'

'I'll walk you to the road. Let me wheel the pram.'

When he returned home, Dulap checked a buzzard with a damaged wing, which he was sure would mend. Then he dug up some potatoes and onions from his small allotment. What was he to do about Imogen and the baby? He didn't doubt he was the father but hoped she could be reconciled with Samuel. It was probably the best solution for all concerned. What had he been thinking of, making love to a married woman? He had never meant to cause such trouble between husband and wife. One consolation was his vigil at the moors; the hen harriers had raised two chicks successfully.

CHAPTER NINETEEN

Susan's visits to Jack were frequent; there was nothing to stop her. The family were occupied with their own lives, and nobody questioned her absences. Jack was putting pressure on her to move in. One afternoon, lying in bed, he started the conversation.

'How long have we been seeing each other? It must be two years. I want to make it official. Leave the farm and come to live with me.'

Susan sat up, hugging her knees.

'I can't, not yet. Is this arrangement so bad? I see you almost every day, and I love being with you. Don't spoil it, Jack.'

'Right,' Jack replied, 'I'll get up then. Got sheep to look after. Busy day ahead. Coffee?'

Nothing more was said. Susan knew it was useless to argue and left. Jack was resentful; when would she leave Peter? Three years, four years? Forcing the issue didn't work. He'd given up a lot of time, without pay, to help Peter run his farm, especially when he fell ill. Well, he might think twice next time he was needed. Susan returned home in a bad mood. She knew Jack's frustration was justified, and she understood how he felt. But, it was complicated; if she left now, would that mean a divorce? All their money had been sunk into the farm, and she would still need her own money. Did she want to depend totally on Jack? Mattie knew about the affair, but Ethan and Peter didn't. How would they take her leaving?

No one was home. Mattie was away on her course, Ethan must be with Dulap, and there was no sign of Peter. She would go to "The

Curlew", have a few drinks and enjoy some company. She knew a few people to talk to, and the landlord was friendly. The family were doing what they wanted; so would she. After a conversation with a few regulars, she got bored and found a table away from the bar after ordering a double gin and tonic. A pleasant way to spend a few hours. After two more drinks, Susan felt lightheaded and was unsteady; it was time to leave. Could she manage, though, without making a fool of herself? Close to the door, standing up, holding onto the chair, Susan looked around, but no one was looking. Walking as steadily as possible, she made it outside. Taking deep breaths and walking slowly, she made it back. Peter was in the yard.

'What's wrong, Susan? Where have you been?'

Susan laughed and, unable to keep her balance, fell. Peter got her up, helping her into the kitchen. Sitting her on a chair, he said, 'You're drunk.'

'Yes, Peter, I'm certainly drunk. Been to the pub. Feel sick. I'm going upstairs.'

'I'll help you.'

'Bugger off, Peter. I don't want any help,' stumbling up the stairs, Susan crawled onto the bed.

Peter had rarely seen his wife in such a state. Once or twice at a wedding, perhaps. Why today? Was going to "The Curlew" the reason she was out so much? What other explanation could there be? Was she so unhappy? He had never questioned Susan about her absences, and she had never confided in him. What should he do about it? No idea unless he turned to Jack. Yes, he'd see his friend. He'd listen; might even advise him.

'Peter, what's wrong?'

'I just need someone to talk to. Do you mind?'

Jack's initial shock at seeing Peter subsided. It was obvious he knew nothing about him and Susan.

'Sure, come in. Sit down, fancy a beer?'

Peter's anxiety lifted. Jack's company was just what he needed. He relaxed.

'I want to talk about Susan. I know it's wrong to do this behind her back, but she came home pretty drunk and collapsed in the yard. Had to help her into the house; she's sleeping it off now. Can't understand what's got into her? I know she goes out most days, never tells me anything, and I never ask. Maybe I don't want to know; she must spend her time in the pub. If this keeps happening, I'll have a real problem on my hands. Why is she doing it, Jack?'

'I don't know. What will you do?'

Peter shook his head.

'I suppose I have taken her for granted. Susan's always been with me, even though the relationship has changed over the years. Look, you're her friend too. Would you talk to her? I'd be really grateful if you would.'

'Of course, I will. I'll pop round in the morning.'

'Perfect, Jack.'

Susan woke the next day with a headache; apart from that, she felt fine. It was ten. A bath, tea and toast is what she wanted. She was drinking her second cup when Jack walked in.

'Jack, I didn't expect you. Does Peter know you're here?'

'He does. In fact, he asked me to come and talk to you because you got drunk yesterday. I'm glad he did; the way we parted was awful.'

'It was, Jack. That's why I ended up in "The Curlew". I was feeling sorry for myself and drank too many gin and tonics. I don't know how I got home. Poor Peter, he was worried when he saw me in that state.'

'Yes, he was and came to me for help. Imagine how I felt, knowing the real reason.'

'Poor you. This is turning into a nightmare; maybe it's time to tell him. The next few days, I promise. It's going to be a terrible shock, being betrayed by his wife and his best friend.'

Jack had a few words with Peter about the farm as he left. Peter came in.

'Feeling better today? Maybe I overreacted a little yesterday, but I was worried about you.'

'You don't have to be, Peter. Whatever you think, I only go to the pub occasionally. People there are so friendly. I get lonely sometimes.'

'Far enough, Susan. I hope you didn't mind me talking to Jack about it. Talking to each other these days seems difficult. I wish it were different.'

'Yes, so do I. We can't return to the time when things were great between us. I still feel tired; I need to lie down for a bit.'

'Wait, Susan; don't go yet. I would like a chat. Just catch up with everything, that's all.'

'If you want, Peter. Is there something special on your mind?'

'Have you heard from Mattie recently?'

'No, not since the last message, which you know about. She's enjoying the practical side of the course, getting out and about, learning all about plants and trees. I really think she's found her calling at last. She went through a bad time, and I'm sorry she lost interest in the farm. I know you had hopes that one day she would take over from you. Are you very disappointed?'

'I was. Now, like you, I'm glad she's happy. A girl like Mattie will have a bright future.'

'She will, Peter. How are things going for you?'

'Now the cows are gone things are easier. Jack's still looking at the diversity opportunities. I don't suppose afternoon teas for tourists appeal to you?'

'Sorry, no. That would mean baking cakes and making sandwiches and pots of tea. I didn't sign up for that. Any other ideas?'

'Maybe Jack will come up with something. The teas were my idea, a silly one, really. Do you think Ethan should worry us? He just spends his days with Dulap, with little thought to the future.'

'He'll find his way,' replied Susan, 'I'm not unduly worried about him.'

'I want to ask you something, Susan. When you agreed to this venture, you said you would leave if it failed. The farm is working and is making a profit. So, does that mean you'll stay now?'

'I'm sorry, I can't promise that. Our marriage is now a friendship, but it's not what I want. I may have to leave.'

'I won't sell the farm, and that includes the house so that I couldn't give you a lot of money. Where could you go?'

'Let's not talk about this now. Mattie comes back next week; let's look forward to that. I'm tired. See you later.'

Peter thought about the situation logically. Susan simply had no other place to go, so he wasn't worried. Once Mattie returned, things would get back to normal, and they would be a unit again. For the moment, the three of them settled down to their respective routines. Susan would not neglect Jack; her visits continued. If Peter noticed, he said nothing.

CHAPTER TWENTY

The rifle was pointing at Bates. Then lowered.

'What the hell! You bastard. Playing games, are you? That's my rifle. You won't intimidate me; no way.'

He started walking towards the figure, who retreated. When Bates reached the spot, the stranger had disappeared. The gamekeeper searched the area. He'd gone.

Bates was sitting in the manager's office when Inspector Parks arrived.

'This is a serious incident. Tell me exactly what happened.'

'It was about seven this morning. I'd been on my usual rounds, checking the feeders and water. I was walking towards the land rover, when I saw someone pointing a rifle right at me. It was my gun, too, stolen from the boot of my vehicle. He was about two hundred feet away. I've seen him before, but, as he's in black clothing, with a balaclava on his face, I don't know who he is.'

'Then what happened?'

'Well, I admit I shouted at him.'

'Not a good idea, sir. The last thing you want in a situation like this is to antagonise him. And then?'

'I walked towards him, but he disappeared. I reckon he knows the area well. All the entrances and exits were easy for him to get away from. I'll not let him get the better of me.'

'I understand the way you feel, Mr Bates, but please don't take the law into your own hands. How long did he point the rifle at you?'

'Not long, a few seconds. Of course, he had no intention of using it, he just wanted to scare me. It won't work, Inspector.'

'Right, I have your statement, and you're sure you don't know who this person could be?'

'I still think it could be Dulap Whottle. I've had trouble with him before, and he's never hidden his dislike of me. Still, it's not his style. He's got some idea in his head that I shoot raptors who nest on the moors, which is not true.'

Inspector Parks had his own views about this, well aware of the gamekeeper's reputation. He knew birds were persecuted. Still, he didn't want people pointing rifles at each other.

'Right then, I have all the information I need for the present. Be sure to let me know if anything else occurs.'

'I'll be sure to, Inspector. Whoever it is must be a nutter.'

The Inspector was relieved to get back into his car. He didn't like Bates. Who did? He had broken the law, killing protected birds and destroying nests. The time would come when he had enough evidence to convict him. Dulap did trespass on the moors; that was well known, but he couldn't be arrested unless there was actual proof. Was he the stranger in black? Doubtful, but not impossible. This rifle incident was unusual for this area. Let's hope there was no more of it.

The black clothes were in a pile, ready to be washed. A balaclava could be destroyed, in case the police made a call, which was doubtful. The rifle was difficult to dispose of but only handled with gloves, so no fingerprints, no bullets either. Leaving it outside the police station was risky; better to throw it in the disused, flooded reservoir a few miles away. The shooting season had passed, so let things settle down before the next move.

Bates wasn't worried about his experience, but his manager was. Something else he had to report, and the owners would not be happy. This time, his headkeeper might be subject to another interview. Not that they cared about the death of a few birds, but the publicity and police involvement were a different matter. Bates was becoming a liability; he'd better watch out.

Mattie returned home. Everyone was pleased to see her.

'Welcome back, darling,' Susan said. 'We all want to hear about your two weeks, when you're ready, of course. Jack would like to hear about your experiences, too. He's coming over later. I thought we could all have supper together. Even Ethan is going to be home. How about that?'

'That's a lovely idea, Mum. I've lots to tell and plenty of course material as well, so you can all read about it. How's everyone been?' Mattie lowered her voice. 'What about you and Jack?'

'The relationship has been under strain lately. Jack wants me to move in with him, which is understandable; it's what I want too. We've known each other for two years now. Things must change.'

Mattie agreed. 'Then, that's what you must do, Mum. You have my support. Of course, it will be tough on Dad, not just about you leaving, but finding out your lover is Jack. I can't believe he hasn't guessed yet. Ethan is a different matter, and he's still immature for his age. Do you remember when he became jealous over Dad's friendship with Dulap? Just because he was working on the farm. You'll only be a few miles away, so he can visit you whenever he wants, and no doubt you'll be popping over here, too.'

'Of course I would, Mattie. Oh, it's so good to talk to you and to know you understand. You've grown up so suddenly. I will need your help with Ethan and your Dad too. It won't be easy.'

'I know, Mum. Ethan's never at home these days. I suppose he spends all his time with Dulap, literally coming home to eat and sleep without talking to any of us. Decide when you want to go, and I'll support you.'

When Ethan came in, Susan tried talking to him.

'Hello, darling, had a good day?'

Getting no response, she continued, 'I asked you a question, Ethan. You don't have to tell me, but don't treat me as though I'm invisible.'

'Yes, it's been a great day. O. k. with that?'

'No, I'm not O.k. with that. I'm interested in your life and what you do. Is that a bad thing, Ethan? Can't we spend a little time together, as mother and son? I'm sure you're very different from

Dulap. Not that I'm blaming him; he's a good friend to you; I just wish you weren't so distant with me.'

Without looking at Susan, Ethan replied, 'Whatever. Don't do supper for me; I had something earlier. Going upstairs now.'

Susan phoned Jack.

'Hey, I've had a wonderful talk with Mattie. She made me realise it was time for a change and a move. I'll come over tomorrow and discuss how to do this.'

She then knocked on Ethan's door.

'I need to speak to you. It's Important.'

He let her in.

'I want you home tomorrow by 5 o'clock at the latest. Can't explain now. Just be here.'

'Why?'

'Please Ethan, just this once, do this for me. It really is important.'

'Right, I'll be home by then.'

The next day, Jack and Susan arrived back together. Peter had been told about the meeting and assumed it was about plans for the farm. Mattie and Ethan were sitting around the table with their father.

'We'll just sit down with you all. I asked Jack to come because it concerns him too. I have decided to leave the farm, not far, just to Jack's.'

'What! Why?' shouted Peter. He looked from Susan to his friend and Susan again. 'Oh, I see now, this is about the pair of you, isn't it? How could I have been so stupid when it was there all the time? You came to help me on the farm, Jack, but never left without spending time with my wife. You bastard! Get out of my house, now.'

'Please, Peter, listen...'

'Get out, Jack.'

'Best to go,' Susan said.

'How long has this been going on then? Now I know why you are out of the house all the time. Not going on walks or the pub, but at Jack's farm.'

Ethan said nothing but gathered a few things in his rucksack and left.

Peter turned to Mattie.

'Why aren't you saying anything unless you knew. That's it, isn't it? Why didn't you tell me?'

'It wasn't up to me, Dad; this is between you and Mum. But I accept it, and I understand. That's the way it is, and nothing will alter it. I can imagine how betrayed you must be feeling and angry. Nobody plans this kind of thing. I'm here for you, too. I love you both.'

Dulap was surprised when Ethan knocked on his door.

'What's up, Lad? You only left an hour ago. You're upset. Come in.'

'Can I stay tonight, Dulap? Mum's leaving us to live with Jack. I can't believe it, how could she? She doesn't care about me.'

'Sit down, Ethan and listen to me. Of course, your Mum loves and cares for you very much. I didn't know about this, but it must be a shock for you.'

'Not Mattie, she knew all about it and said nothing.'

'I expect Susan needed someone to confide in, and they seem to be close. Be honest, Ethan, when was the last time you sat down and had a real heart-to-heart with either of your parents? You talk to me all the time, tell me your troubles, thoughts and feelings, and I'm glad you do, so I can be there when you need me. You're a young man now, not a child. Maybe you should try to understand how everyone's feeling right now. I think your Dad needs your support, maybe he's on his own wanting to talk to someone. Try not to take sides, though and talk about your Mum. Remain loyal to them both. You can stay as long as you need to. I'll make up a bed. Hungry?'

Dulap's reasoning did not convince Ethan, but he was glad of a few days away, giving him time to think about it. He phoned Peter and let him know where he was, borrowed pyjamas from Dulap, and felt better. He would see his Mum, but for now just wanted to hide away.

Dulap thought about Imogen and the baby. What was her name? Would he see them again? He missed her, the lovely face and gentle ways. What if she moved with Samuel? Well, it wasn't up to him. At the moment he had his duty to Ethan, guiding him with his conflicting emotions. He wandered outside, lit his pipe, sat for a while and then checked his allotment before going in. He was certainly feeling his age tonight.

CHAPTER TWENTY ONE

Mona hadn't expected too much from online dating. The first man she met spent the whole time talking about his dead wife. While understanding how much he must miss her, she didn't appreciate having made the effort to see him, only to sit opposite someone who had no interest in her at all. After an hour, she made her excuses and left. Why had he bothered? She waited a few weeks before trying again. This time, the man she met looked nothing like his picture, in looks or age. She was quickly bored in his company and escaped.

'It was awful,' Mona told Leona. 'Maybe the best men have been snapped up. I'll keep going with it for a while, just see how it goes. There must be someone decent out there. Maybe the secret is not to expect too much. We'll see.'

A week later, she checked her account and found a picture and message.

'What do you think of this one?'

'Let's look. Oh, Darnley, I like the name. He has a nice, open face. Never been married, I wonder why? Six feet tall and a soil scientist, whatever that is. Are you going to arrange a meeting, dear?'

'Yes, Leona, I'll take a chance. He lives in Lincolnshire, but will drive here. I'll suggest a meeting in "The Curlew" on Saturday at noon.'

On the day, Mona arrived early; just before Darnley walked in. He was a large man, and, although not fat, he showed his appetite for food and drink and life. People rarely forgot their first meeting with him, for his personality was no less memorable. Confident and knowledgeable on many subjects, he rarely lost an argument and would not readily own up when he did. He could be dogmatic and overpowering, but was also kind and generous. People liked and disliked him in equal measures.

'Mona, nice to meet you. What can I get you to drink?'

'A pint of lager, please; no special kind. Thank you.'

'A larger it is then. Hungry? I'll bring the menu over, no rush to eat. Just when you like.'

Mona liked Darnley, but she reminded herself that this was the first meeting; she knew nothing about him.

'You come from Lincolnshire. A bit of a journey.'

'No problem at all, Mona. I enjoy driving, and I'm used to travelling with my job. Besides, I liked your profile and decided that I would like to meet you.'

'That's a nice thing to say, Darnley. You're a soil scientist. What do you do exactly?'

'Well, soil is a natural resource, which includes its chemical, biological and physical aspects, particularly in its use and management. I worked for a time in improving land for the

production of food by studying land degradation and how to improve
the soil. My last job was in the States, helping farmers to get the best
out of their land, depending on whether they wanted to grow crops or
keep livestock.'

'Is this just a holiday, or are you back to stay?' Mona asked.

'I'm here to stay. I enjoyed my time over there, but now I want
to settle down — that's the reason I joined the dating site. I hope to
find a woman to share my life with. Children would be nice, too.'

'Well,' replied Mona, 'I've been married, but I'm on good terms
with my ex-husband now, which is good for my daughter, Mollie. We
live with my dear friend, Leona, who literally invited us to stay with
her one day, knowing little about us. I owe her so much. If you get to
meet her, you'll see what an incredible person she is. I don't work,
preferring to be there for Mollie while she is young. Leona refuses to
accept money from me in the way of rent or bills, but I help with the
cost of food. She is a professional clairvoyant, although she doesn't
practice anymore.'

'That's interesting. Tell me, have you ever visited Lincolnshire?'

'No, I haven't. I know, it's an agricultural county with fields of
potatoes and other crops.'

Darnley laughed. 'Absolutely right there. But there's another side
to it; there's the Lincolnshire Wolds, a little-known area of
outstanding beauty. Gentle green hills and valleys and so much more.
The rocks interest me: sandstone, chalk and limestone, formed in the

Cretaceous period, 140-65 million years ago. Sorry, I get carried away by my passion for geology.'

'Please don't apologise, Darnley, you are not boring me. In fact, I am enjoying myself immensely.'

'Glad to hear it. Now, how about we eat? Choose what you want while I get another round. I'll have to have a soft drink; I'm driving.'

After the meal, Darnley suggested a walk around the village. As they strolled, he said, 'I would like to see you again, Mona, If you are of a like mind. Can I suggest a visit to one of my favourite places? I live in the Lincolnshire Wolds, which is near a town called Louth, where we could have lunch. After that, a trip to the coast. Can you make it next Saturday?'

When Mona returned home, she told Leona about the meeting and the plans for the weekend.

'That's nice, Mona, but be careful, and I want you to call me when you get there.'

'I will, don't worry. I have a good feeling about him.'

Saturday was a mixture of light showers and sunny patches. Mona was ready by nine, and Darnley arrived on time. She slept for half of the journey, something she always did on a long drive.

'How about we stop for a coffee? There's a cafe over there,' Darnley suggested.

'Yes, maybe it will wake me up properly.'

After Lunch, they headed for the Lincolnshire coast.

'We'll go to Saltfleetby and Theddlethorpe Dunes,' Darnley said. 'It's an interesting place because the sand there is extremely fine and blows onto the land to form new dunes. Lots of plants and flowers, as well as bees and butterflies, and a host of other insects. Many species of birds, too. There used to be a bombing practice site there, but thankfully, that's moved to Donna Nook.'

The day had turned bright, with a slight breeze, as they arrived at the long, shady shore, backed by saltwater marshes, which gave way to mudflats and sands and freshwater behind that. Darnley searched about in the water.

'This is meadowsweet, with their erect and leafy stems. It grows in profusion here. Its other name is meadwort.'

Mona looked at the tall, reddish stems and the delicate, creamy-white flowers.

'They have a strange, sweet smell.'

Darnley nodded. 'Yes, they do. In the past, the flowers were picked, then dried and used to cover floors to sweeten the air. They have an almost antiseptic quality.'

They moved on to the edge of the salt marshes, where thrift grew in abundance, forming a dense, springy cover. The small, rounded heads, pink and sweetly scented, were still in bloom. He pointed out the sea purslane that covered the marsh, forming masses of dense grey patches with their grey leaves.

On the landward side, the dunes were old and stable. They continued to walk, passing viper's bugloss, sea couch and prickly buckthorn, which covered much of the dunes, providing cover and nesting sites for waders, meadow pipits and skylarks.

For a while, Mona and Darnley stood side-by-side, looking at the wide expanse of the coastal landscape before them, and the woodland, hedges and fields which fringed them. Then, without a word, Darnley took Mona's hand, leading her back to the car.

CHAPTER TWENTY TWO

Dulap made a coffee, then walked outside, sitting on the old wicker chair inherited from his parents, like everything he owned. As much as he enjoyed Ethan's visits, he relished the time on his own. Finishing his drink, he wandered over to his vegetable garden. The board beans were finished; they had been excellent this year. Plenty of potatoes to dig up, runner beans and sweet peas to pick. A patch of dahlias looked bright and colourful, in various types and shades of pinks, reds, yellows and white.

He went inside and made an omelette. A tap on the door startled him. He doubted it was Ethan, as he always walked in.

'I'm sorry to come, but I had to get away from him. It has become unbearable at the vicarage. I didn't know what else to do?'

Imogen stood in the doorway in tears. The baby was asleep in her pram. Underneath that was a large bag, hastily packed.

'Imogen, lass, come in, you're shaking and upset. Sit down on the sofa. I'll make a cup of tea, then you can tell me about it.'

'Oh, thank you, Dulap. Do you have a tissue? I must look a real fright. Things are so bad at home; Samuel nags me constantly, even when I'm with Iris. I can be changing her nappy, feeding her, or just having a cuddle. He asks me repeatedly if she is his child? I've begged him to stop, but he won't, and well, in the end, I told him the truth, that you are her father. Please, can we stay with you, where I feel loved and safe? Don't make me go back to him.'

'Hey, it's fine, lass, don't worry. I've had you both on my mind; I love her name, by the way. I can hardly believe you are here with me. Of course, if this is what you truly want, you can stay here for as long as you like. I'll not send you away. How about I get a pillow, so you lay here and rest, or sleep? We may likely get a visit from Samuel, but I'll be here. You won't have to see him at all unless you want to. We'll talk later when you feel up to it. Best to make the most of it while the little one sleeps.'

While Imogen slept, he put fresh linen on the bed and made sure everything was dusted and tidy; a jar filled with wildflowers was placed on the bedside table. After taking a peek at Iris, he sat outside. He suspected their marriage had never been an easy one or particularly loving. Dulap couldn't really understand why such a lovely woman would turn to himself to find love and companionship, but the passion had come so naturally to both of them, the difference in their ages no barrier. She may not stay, and he would accept that, but he hoped that her being with him was more than just an escape.

An hour passed, and he heard the baby's cry. Opening the door slowly, he saw Imogen popped up on the pillow, feeding Iris. She looked around and smiled, motioning Dulap to come in.

'You seem better, lass. How do you feel now?'

'Much better, just being here with you and Iris. Like a proper family.'

'Just be sure this is what you want? Look around you, lass. All I can offer is a small, run-down cottage. I have a pleasant garden and allotment, surrounded by trees, but not the large house and garden you have been used to. I will certainly make repairs and changes to make life comfortable for you. It just needs some homely touches that you might care to do. Whatever I have, is yours.'

'This is where I want to be, Dulap. Give me a few days and just see what I can do. I will have to make a few trips to the vicarage; there are clothes for Iris and me personal items, and I have spare curtains and bedding, which will brighten the cottage. The best day to go will be Sunday morning; Samuel is never at home then.'

'I'll have to come with you. I can carry so much more, and you will have to look after Iris. In fact, I have an old cart with handles, which is serviceable. Make a list of everything you want to bring back. Is there anything you need now? Nappies, wipes? I can quickly nip to the shop now.'

'Yes, a few things to tide me over. I can get the baby bath on Sunday, but for now, a large washing-up bowl will do nicely.'

'Right, let's have the list, and I'll go now. I'll find something for supper. Lock the door while you're on your own, and don't let anyone in. Won't be long.'

Imogen lent back on the high-backed sofa; Iris had fallen to sleep in her arms. A slow contentment crept into her being, and she had forgotten how that felt. Anxiety and fear had been her companions for so long.

The door handle turned, and she heard the rattle of someone trying to get in. Then a loud knocking on the door, then the window.

'Dulap, it's me, Ethan. Open up.'

Imogen sensed a face at the window. She stiffened and looked at Iris, still sleeping. Whoever it is must give up and go soon. Ethan tried the back door, which was locked as well. He always came about this time, so if Dulap were going to be out, he would leave him a note on the front door. What was he playing at? Well, he wouldn't hang around or come back later. He'd try tomorrow. Should he go home? No, he'd see Mum. He didn't want to meet Jack but would have to face him sometime. Besides, he was hungry.

On his way, Ethan passed the church and remembered there was a shortcut through the churchyard. He was halfway along it when a tall man he had never seen before was walking the other way towards him. His appearance shocked Ethan; his eyes were red and swollen, and misery clouded his face.

'Hello,' Samuel said, 'are you just walking through?'

'Yes, I'm on my way to see my Mum.'

Ethan wanted to walk on, but his way was blocked; this man wanted to talk.

'I see. I'm going to the church. My name's Samuel, and I'm the vicar here. You seem a little agitated. Can I be of any help to you?'

'No, it's nothing, just disappointed. My friend wasn't home when I called. Dulap usually lets me know when he's going to be out.'

'Dulap! You say he's your friend?'

'Yes', replied Ethan, 'What's it to you? Anyway, I must go now.'

Samuel put his arm onto Ethan's shoulder.

'Wait, just a minute. Was anyone else there?'

'No, why should there be? Lives on his own, always has.'

Ethan pushed past Samuel. Looking back, he saw the man looking in his direction.

Knocking on the farm door, Susan answered it.

'Ethan, what a pleasant surprise. Come in.'

'Hi, Mum, I've just called at Dulap's, but he wasn't home. I didn't wait, so I decided to see how you're doing. Where's Jack?'

'Oh, around somewhere. I'm glad you're here. Stay for lunch. Ready in about an hour.'

'Great. As I was walking through the path, by the church, a strange thing happened. The vicar stopped me, and I think he just wanted someone to talk to. He looked as though he'd been crying. Seemed a bit spaced out to me. Anyway, I mentioned Dulap, and he went crazy.'

'Yes, that does sound strange. Mind you, there was a sort of rumour going around the village about his wife, but I know nothing about that. Can't see what that's got to do with Dulap? Just a domestic problem, I expect. Now, you realise Jack will be in for his lunch? Is that a problem?'

Ethan shrugged. 'No, not really. I'll have to get used to it; I always liked him. To be honest, Dulap put me straight on several things.'

'I'm glad, Ethan. How's your dad? I think about him. I've seen little of him or Mattie. You know, talking of Mattie; she could really help you. You used to be so close, you could talk to her about anything. Will you see Dulap tomorrow?'

'Sure, he can't be out twice in a row; he must be expecting me.'

Jack came in, surprised and pleased to see Ethan, although not sure what to say.

'Well, lunch is ready,' Susan said, 'happens to be your favourite, Ethan, shepherd's pie. I know the situation is a little difficult at the moment, but I really want you two to get on.'

'I'm willing to try, Ethan. How about you? We always did before. I realise you may not feel the same way now.'

'It's fine, Jack,' Ethan replied, 'I was angry initially, you can understand that, but now I accept the situation. I just feel so sad for Dad. Thanks for the meal, Mum. Great, as always. I'd better get back after this.'

The next day, Ethan walked to Dulap's. The door was open, so he walked in. Imogen was bathing Iris in the washing-up bowl.

'Hello, you must be Ethan? Glad to meet you, I'm Imogen.'

'Where's Dulap?'

'I think Dulap had better explain. He's coming downstairs now.'

'Hey, Ethan, let's talk outside so that I can explain the situation.'

'Fine by me.'

'Let's sit here, lad. Imogen has moved in with me. I hope it lasts, but I've not much control over that. We met a while ago; it was clear she needed a friend, someone to talk to. After a while, we became lovers. She's married to the vicar, but I'm the baby's father. I love her, Ethan. I don't know if she loves me, but her being here is enough.'

'I can't believe this. You never mentioned her to me, not once.'

'I didn't, Ethan, because I have a right to my privacy. I wanted to keep things to myself until I knew what would happen. Imogen needs time to settle in, and I hope you get to like her. That doesn't mean we can't still do things together, like before, just not as frequently.'

'Well, that's just fine, Dulap,' Ethan said sarcastically, 'do what you like. Call me when you're ready to meet. I'm going home.'

'Is everything all right, Dulap?' Imogen asked. 'It sounds as though your friend wasn't too happy.'

'He'll come around, but he must understand that things have changed, and he needs to adjust accordingly. My priority right now is you and Iris. I hope Ethan and I can still be good friends.'

Ethan arrived home and found Mattie in the kitchen.

'Hello, Ethan, been with Dulap?'

'You could say that. Know what he's done? There's a young woman with a baby living with him. A right cosy set-up. According to him, he's the father. I know who her husband is. Get this, Mattie, the vicar.'

'You're joking, Ethan. How do you know?'

'Because yesterday, I passed this man on my way to see Mum. He seemed lonely and wanted to chat. When I told him I'd been to see Dulap, he freaked out; he must have been the vicar. Anyway, I can't be doing all that just now. It was nice to see Mum and Jack, and I have come to an understanding with him. Anything for lunch? Where's Dad?'

'He's having a bath. I gave him some of my special bath salts, and he's having a relaxing soak. He doesn't seem as down as he was a few days ago.'

Ethan managed a smile.

'I'm glad about that. I'd really like a talk with you sometime, Mattie. Things have changed so much lately, and I feel I should do the same. I'd appreciate your advice.'

'I'm so glad you feel this way. How about over the weekend? I've got details of dozens of courses you may be interested in.'

On Sunday morning, Dulap and Imogen went to the vicarage and got everything she needed, including the baby bath. She found the curtains she was looking for, a flowery pair for the living-room and some bright-blue ones for the bedroom. There was a smaller bedroom in the cottage, which would become a room for Iris. It took two trips to collect everything, including the cot, rug and a small chest of drawers.

Imogen was relieved when it was done, and she was safely back in the cottage. She feared Samuel, and what he might do when he realised she was gone for good.

CHAPTER TWENTY THREE

It shocked the congregation at the morning service to see their vicar looking so ill. When he rose to give the blessing, there were audible gasps and meaningful glances within the pews. Samuel seemed in a trance-like state. The curate conducted most of the service, apart from the communion, which Samuel had to administer. There was no sermon, and everyone was relieved when it was all over.

The two churchwardens agreed to hold a meeting with the rest of the committee to discuss what should be done. The vicar could hardly function and couldn't perform his duties properly. Above all, he needed help and understanding.

One warden, Arthur Westlake, began. 'Thank you all for coming at such short notice. We all know of the strain that our vicar has been under lately. Unfortunately, it has proved impossible to stop the gossip about his private life, but we are here today to decide how to help our minister and friend.'

A retired vicar, Nathaniel Mabbs, gave his assurance that he would take over Samuel's duties for the time being.

Audrey Miles, the second churchwarden said, 'Thank you, Nathaniel. It is a relief to know church life will continue as normal. Now, Arthur and I think the Bishop should be informed of recent events. I am happy to contact him and will keep you all up-to-date with developments.'

'I believe Samuel went to his Lordship recently to request a relocation,' added Mr Flowers, the treasurer. 'Can anyone confirm this?'

'Yes, that's right,' replied Audrey. 'I understand it was because of problems within his marriage. He was happy when he first came here, and I thought them a perfect couple, but, well, something changed.'

'Has anyone seen Imogen lately?' Nathaniel asked. 'I heard she had given birth, which, if true, should be something to celebrate.'

'Who told you?' Audrey asked.

'One of our dear ladies, who arrange the flowers. She met Imogen, wheeling a pram. A little girl, apparently. That's all I can tell you. All strange. Anyway, we will be advised by his Lordship and place the matter in his hands.'

Samuel was unaware of the concern he was causing. He knew he wasn't fully competent in performing his work, but once his dear wife came back to him, all would be well again. In fact, he was going to find and bring her home. Just a little persuasion on his part was all that was needed to achieve this. He found out where Dulap's cottage was, banged on his door and then forced his way in.

'Get out of my way. I want to see my wife and take her back to the vicarage, where she belongs. Where is she?'

Imogen came from the kitchen. 'Samuel! Please, calm down. You don't look well. Sit down, and we can talk.'

'I'll be outside,' Dulap said.

Her husband's appearance alarmed Imogen. His normally clear, blue eyes were blood-shot and seemed sunk into his face. He was unshaven, with hair unbrushed and clothes unwashed. Samuel looked at her and realised his mission was hopeless. She looked so happy, wearing her favourite yellow dress. Iris was asleep in the cot.

'Tell me, my dear, would you have left me if you knew the baby was mine?'

'Yes, Samuel, maybe not as soon, but I would eventually have gone. I'm so sorry; I hate to see you like this.'

'I need your company, Imogen. I don't know what's happening to me. The bishop is coming to see me. Can you believe that? Apparently, Audrey phoned him without a mention of it to me. I have been doing my ministerial duties, as always. I can't understand any of it.'

'Samuel, dear, that's just it; you haven't been doing that. You are unwell, and that's why the church committee have taken the tough decisions they have. When you see the bishop, try to be honest with him. I will come back and stay for a few days, but please realise that I can't stay and live there as before.'

'Oh, thank you, my dear, thank you.' Samuel slumped forward and would have fallen onto the floor if Imogen hadn't caught him.

Dulap helped to lay him on the bed, covering the silent figure with a throw.

'I will have to go back and look after him, Dulap. You understand, don't you? It won't be for long; he needs professional medical help.'

Dulap hugged Imogen. 'I don't like it, but do whatever is needed to get Samuel through this terrible time. Come and see me when you can. Just keep me informed. Can you walk him home later without my help?'

'Yes, if you could bring some things back, which I will need. I'll write a list. You can drop them off later. Thank you, my love.'

Towards evening, Imogen had returned to her former home, with baby Iris. Samuel let her put him to bed. His wife was back, and now he could sleep. His world looked brighter, and he would even accept Iris as his own. Everything would be as it used to be.

Imogen made up a bed in the spare room, then went down to clean the kitchen and living room, which had been neglected. Suddenly, she stopped as if in a trance; she listened to the lonely, beautiful song of the blackbird, feeling her with joy and yet a strange sadness. The space and comfort of the vicarage had lost much of its appeal to her. Still, she sat in her favourite chair and fed Iris. It was the garden she missed. The roses were still flowering well, the deep red clusters of the "Rose De Rescht", with its wonderful fragrance, and a yellow potted rose, kept just outside the door, with its rich, lemon scent. It all needed attention from her. Maybe tomorrow, she would spend the morning dead-heading and tidying up the borders. A flood of resentment then flooded over Imogen but was tempered by concern over Samuel. She considered the situation. Samuel was mentally unstable and couldn't be left on his own. Maybe he should be in the hospital? She didn't want to be the person to make that decision. See how he was in the morning and try to talk to him? Maybe discuss the options? Also, call Audrey and ask her to call around as soon as possible.

Iris was crying. Now, all her concern was for her baby; for the moment, nothing else mattered.

The next day, Imogen phoned Audrey. 'Hello, it's Imogen. I really need to consult you. I'm at the vicarage, looking after Samuel, but I haven't moved back permanently. He's doing nothing for himself. He needs professional help.'

'I don't quite understand. Are you saying you have left him? The marriage is over?'

'Yes, Audrey, the vicarage isn't my home anymore. I care about Samuel, but I'm out of my depth.'

'Right then, the best thing will be for me to call around, see Samuel and go from there. I will need a set of keys to have access to the vicarage in case you are not always there.'

'Of course,' replied Imogen, 'when could you come?'

'I have a few rounds to make, but I can be with you by twelve.'

The matter was settled, bringing great relief to Imogen. She bought Samuel tea. He was awake and so pleased to see her.

'How do you feel, Samuel? Drink this. You should eat something, won't take me long to make it.'

The vicar smiled. 'I'm so glad to see you, my dear. Are you back to stay? Please say you are.'

'We can talk about that later. I can hear Iris crying. I must go.'

'Iris?'

'Yes, my baby, Samuel. Of course, I brought her with me. I expect she needs a feed or a nappy change. I'll return with your breakfast as soon as I can.'

'I remember now, Imogen. Baby Iris, of course. May I see her? I can be a father to her, you know. Give me another chance, my dear.'

'Of course, you can see her, but I must go now.'

Imogen was relieved to make her escape. Iris was asleep in her cot, just as she had been for the last hour. As she prepared the food, thoughts crowded in her mind for attention. Should Samuel be told about Audrey's visit? No, he might object. Better for her to come unannounced, so she could see how things were for herself.

'Sit up, Samuel. I've made scrambled eggs, your favourite. After breakfast, maybe a shower and a change of clothing?'

'Yes, whatever you say, my dear. Are you going out?'

'Not at the moment. Don't worry.'

Audrey arrived. Imogen made coffee and explained the situation.

'Unfortunately, things are not how Samuel wants them to be. I don't have the heart to tell him the marriage is really over. I'm so grateful to you for coming.'

'I'm fond of Samuel; we all are,' Audrey replied, 'it's part of my job to look after the welfare of all church members, including the vicar. Is he expecting me?'

'No, I thought it best not to tell him. He doesn't seem aware of reality, and he won't know why you have come. I'll take you to see him.'

Samuel had showered and was looking out of the window, his eyes not focused on anything. Hearing the door open, he turned around.

'Audrey, what are you doing here? Is anything wrong?'

Audrey smiled and said, 'I haven't seen you for a while, vicar. I came to see how you are.'

'What do you mean? I took the service only last Sunday...surely...I remember... I feel so tired...so tired.'

The two women exchanged a glance.

'Do you want to talk to him on your own?' Imogen asked.

'No, I can see how it is. I'll wait downstairs and discuss what can be done for him.'

Imogen helped Samuel back to bed and took his hand.

'Maybe you will sleep for a while. I'll be up later.'

'He's not himself at all, is he?' said Audrey. 'From my experience, I would say he has suffered a breakdown. He needs to see a doctor who can prescribe medicine and perhaps refer him to the hospital; they have an excellent mental health department there. If you can contact the surgery, I will inform the bishop. I'm not sure a visit from his Lordship is the best action right now.' She paused, then asked, 'Is there any chance of a reconciliation? I know it's not my business, but...'

'No, I've moved on; things have changed for me. I'll do all I can for Samuel and will stay here for the time being, but I will have to go, eventually. Thank you so much for your help. I'll be in touch soon.'

The patient was sleeping, so Imogen put Iris into her pram and walked to the cottage. Dulap was in. They hugged.

'I will have to go back soon, but I have the support of Audrey, a churchwarden, and I'm going to get medical help for Samuel. We just have to be patient. I'll come tomorrow if I can. I love you.'

'I understand, lass. I'll wait in for you.'

When Imogen returned, she found Samuel searching the house frantically. He wept with relief when he saw her.

'Imogen, where have you been? I thought you had gone again. I can't live without you; I'd rather die.'

She sat him down in the living room.

'I'm here for you, Samuel, to help you get better. You must see a doctor. You will, won't you, for me?'

Samuel looked at his wife. 'I will do whatever you say, my dear. As long as you are with me.'

CHAPTER TWENTY FOUR

Ethan's relationship with Dulap had changed. He missed his friend, whose life was increasingly taken up with Imogen and Iris. Still, he hoped there would be a time in the future for walks on the moors and fighting the common enemy. Today, he went there anyway, just to see what, if anything, was going on. As he walked, his anger towards Dulap surfaced. He'd stopped caring about the birds he had promised to love and protect. Foolish old man, getting involved with a woman half his age and landing himself with a baby. She won't stay with him. Then, when he was alone again, with time to reflect on his genuine friends, he'd come crawling back.

The morning was bright and warm, which comforted the young man. Wispy streaks of clouds floated in the expanse of blue overhead. It was so still; an air of expectancy hung in the air. Should he carry on on his own? Just for a short way, have a look around. He noticed a wire circled around to make a snare, a trap for any unsuspecting animal, like a fox, cat, stoat or even a small dog. Ethan collected four more and felt pleased with himself. After stuffing them into his rucksack, he walked on, making his way to the site of a known harrier nesting site. A falcon trap was placed carefully nearby, partially covered with heather. Totally illegal, but it could still be bought or made by an experienced gamekeeper. Of course, the birds could be released but rarely were.

It was clouding over. Ethan wanted to go back to the safety of the woods. Maybe he'd see his Mum. It started to rain heavily. Sitting out of sight, under a tree with a broad canopy, he waited. The flask of tea and egg sandwiches were a comfort.

An hour passed, and the downpour continued. Ethan stood up and stretched his legs. Packing everything away, he walked back to the road. The swiftly moving clouds were grey, and Ethan was wet and cold. There was something on the side of the path, a tawny owl, absolutely sodden, caught out in the heavy rain. Should he pick it up? He knew these birds could be aggressive; people had been attacked and badly injured, even losing an eye. He bent down to look closer. This one was so wet it couldn't fly and looked exhausted. Ethan opened his jacket and put the owl inside. There was only one thing he could do now: go to Dulap's cottage. He'd know what to do.

Dulap was home. Ethan handed the owl to him and then stepped into the warm interior of the living room.

'I'm glad you brought her to me, Ethan. The feathers are completely waterlogged. I'll dry her with a towel.'

The owl remained still, with her eyes closed, traumatised by the experience. With the warmth of the room, her feathers dried, becoming soft and feathery again. While she remained docile, Dulap examined her. He stroked the large, round head and her rufous, brown-stripped, mottled plumage. He whispered to her. The owl seemed to study them both, with her black eyes set within the large facial disks. The thin, "extra eyebrows" set on each side of the dark strip, running down to the bill, gave her the typical "kindly expression" of her kind.

Ethan stayed, drinking hot chocolate, while he waited for the owl's recovery. He was feeling guilty for his previous bad feelings about Dulap, feeling glad for his company again.

'Where did you find her, lad?'

'I was walking back from the moors. I'd decided to have a snoop around, and I'm glad I did. Look at these.' He opened his rucksack, giving Dulap the trap and snares.

'Well, what do we have here?' Dulap said. 'You did well to find these. Nothing caught in them?'

'No, thank goodness. I'm so glad I found the owl. She wouldn't have survived if Bates had found her.'

'You're right there, Ethan. She'll be dry soon, and you can have the pleasure of releasing her. Listen, I'm sorry I haven't been out much lately. I miss our meetings. I'll make up for it soon, I promise.'

'I'd like that, Dulap, I really would.'

Later, they watched the owl drift away on soft, noiseless wings. Ethan went home feeling happier than he had been for weeks.

'We're glad you came home early, Ethan,' Mattie said, 'did you see Dulap? You haven't mentioned him lately.'

'Yes, I did, but I hadn't planned to. Somehow, the friendship with him seemed to lose its importance. Not that I wanted that. In fact, it made me unhappy. He seemed to have shut me out because of Imogen and the baby. Anyway, I'd been on the moors just to have a look around, and I found wire traps, which I collected. When I started out this morning, it was sunny, but towards mid-morning, it absolutely poured down. I was really wet and decided to come home as quickly as I could. Then I saw something just on the grass verge. You'll never guess what it was?'

'Come on, tell us,' Peter said.

'A tawny owl, and so wet, she couldn't fly off. I put her inside my jacket and went to Dulap's. If there's one person who would know what to do, it's him. He dried her off as best he could and then left her to dry completely. It was amazing how calm she was. I'm sure she was aware she was being helped. It took a while, but eventually, her feathers became fluffy again. Dulap picked her up, and once we were outside, he gave her to me, and I let her go.'

'You lucky thing,' said Mattie, 'I'd love to have an experience like that. I remember once coming across a female sparrowhawk eating a wood pigeon she had just caught. Of course, as soon as she saw me, she was off, with her prey. Still, it was one of those moments when all your senses are focused on that one experience, and you are truly living in the moment.'

'You feel better about Dulap now?' Peter asked.

'Yes, much better. It was the owl which brought us back together. I really believe that however silly it sounds.'

'That's a lovely thought, Ethan,' Mattie replied, 'will you see each now, like before?'

'Maybe not as often, but regularly anyway. Imogen wasn't there today; apparently, she is looking after her husband, who is ill and needs medical help. Dulap is all right about it. She is coming back, and, of course, there's the baby, Iris, Dulap's daughter. I can see he needs to be there for them.'

'Who would have thought it?' Peter said. 'Still, that's all good. Guess what I've made for supper today? Fish pie and peas. I hope you're hungry, Ethan?'

'Starving, Dad. How's everything going with the farm?'

'I'm struggling a bit, and I miss your mother a lot, but I'm getting there. Can't see Jack yet; I think it will be a long time before I do. I still have you two, so life isn't too bad. Right, let's eat.'

Left alone, Dulap thought about Ethan's visit and the owl which had helped to reconcile them. If only Imogen would come back. No doubt Samuel needed help, but the man would say anything to keep her there, including saying he would kill himself. Was it possible she could be persuaded to stay? Surely not, but could he be sure? Damn the man! He had sympathy with his situation, but eventually, he would have to face facts. His marriage was finished, he must let Imogen go. She said she would visit tomorrow when she could get away.

A doctor had been called to see Samuel, as he was incapable of going to the surgery and was threatening suicide if Imogen left him again. The crisis team had been alerted, and Imogen had agreed that her husband should be hospitalised and given all the help he needed.

However, she did not go with him but said she would visit as soon as possible. She had Iris to care for.

When she closed the vicarage door, the relief was overwhelming, and a terrible burden lifted from her. She spent the night there and, in the morning, made her way to the cottage.

'Whatever happens now, I am back to stay, Dulap. Samuel's in hospital and will receive specialist care. I've heard it's an excellent unit. The staff are used to dealing with patients who have Samuel's problems. Of course, I feel so sorry for him, but I am sure he will recover. What else can I do? Your daughter needs a cuddle from her father, and I'm exhausted. Let's have a cup of tea together, and then I'll go for a lie-down. I'll express some milk and put it in the fridge. Don't forget to warm it first.'

Dulap sat down, holding Iris in his arms. She was so beautiful, and his own daughter. Imogen was back, and he felt blessed. He thought of Samuel, his pain, misery and confusion, probably unaware of what was happening.

The process of getting Samuel back to full health was going to be a long and difficult process. There would be periods of confusion, mixed with outbursts of uncontrollable emotion and anger, railing at his wife and Dulap. Drugs helped at these times, and blessed sleep gave him hours of wonderful oblivion. Counselling would come later, much later. He would never go back to his former home. The bishop was aware of the problems, and when Samuel was well enough to leave the hospital, he would help him move on. But that would not be soon.

CHAPTER TWENTY FIVE

Mona's romance was going well. She spent most weekends with Darnley; Leona was happy for her to use the car whenever she wanted, but she rarely used it herself. Despite this, Mona wanted to take things slowly; she had Mollie to think of and was content to carry on as they were for the present. Darnley was ready to move on quickly, to consider marriage, and for Mona and Mollie to move to Lincolnshire.

As always, Mona drew comfort and reassurance from her friend.

'You look worried, my dear. Want to talk?'

'Yes, I do, Leona. You can guess what about. It's Darnley. I love him, but I want to keep things as they are for now.'

'I see. That's not what Darnley wants, though?'

Mona sighed. 'No, and that's the problem. He's even been talking about marriage, and although I'm not opposed to the idea, it's not so easy for me. I'd have to uproot Mollie from her home, her school and friends, let alone Malcolm, not forgetting you, Leona.'

'Don't concern yourself about me, my dear. I can always come and stay, and you can both visit here whenever you want,'

'Bless you, I know that. Darnley's only met Mollie once, and it's not enough for them to get to know each other.'

'That's very true,' replied Leona, 'you will need to talk to Mollie about your feelings for Darnley. Just be honest about it. Make her understand she can still see Malcolm, as before. Christmas will come soon, and perhaps you could invite him over then? One thing at a time. Mollie is a sensible girl; she'll understand more than you think.'

'Thank you, Leona, I'll do that. This weekend will be for me and Mollie. I can always see him during the week.'

Leona clapped her hands. 'Now, I have a confession to make. About two weeks ago, I had a feeling that my old powers had not completely gone, and I was right. It's not as before, but I get glimpses, enough to make a partial reading. Before you say anything, I think you and Darnley have a wonderful future together, but something will happen which will test you.'

'Goodness me, what?'

'I truly do not know; it was not revealed to me. I tried repeatedly, but it was no use. However, the reading was positive. Maybe I shouldn't have told you?'

'No, Leona, you did the right thing. Whatever it is, it can't be that bad, surely? Will you have clients again?'

'Absolutely not. My powers aren't strong now, and I wouldn't want the stress of seeing people again. Now, I'm going to have a spell in the garden. There are a few jobs to do. I'll order some bulbs for the Spring too, maybe some tulips and iris.'

The weekend came and went without Mona talking to Mollie. She felt agitated and didn't like the way she felt.

Darnley's mother paid a visit to her son. She was a lively, positive woman who was delighted by recent developments. Her husband had died some years ago, but she still missed him.

'Well now, darling. Tell me about Mona. You say she has a daughter, Mollie. How old is she?'

'Nine, in December. I have met her once. We seemed to take to each other. Mona really is the woman for me. I've waited a long time to meet her.'

'That's wonderful. Are you ready to settle down then, after all your years abroad? What does Mona think about it?'

'The same as me, but...well, she wants to take things more slowly than I do. We love each other, so why not get on with it?'

Dora reflected. 'Take my advice, try to curb your impatience; otherwise, it might cause trouble — you could lose her. Don't forget she has Mollie to consider, and if they move here, as I expect they would, there will be a lot of adjustments for them both. You see Mona often?'

'Most weekends. Mollie visits her father, Malcolm. I don't know whether he knows about me yet?'

'Well, I would certainly like to meet both of them soon, just when it suits you both.'

'That would be nice, Mum. Mona's spending time with Mollie this weekend, so maybe the following one? She lives with a friend, Leona. An interesting woman. I think you would like her.'

'That all sounds very positive, Darnley. How's the work going?'

'Fine. I do most of it at home. I'd rather work in the field, hands-on. Still, it's well paid, and I'm happy with it for now. Stay the night? I could do with the company.'

'Of course, I can, nothing I'd like better. It also means you can pour me a double gin and tonic. Let's go outside and relax.'

Mona decided it was time to talk to Malcolm, so she called around.

'Mona, how nice to see you. Nothing wrong with Mollie, is there?'

'No, she's fine. I wanted to tell you I've started a relationship. His name's Darnley. He lives in Lincolnshire, has never been married and doesn't have children. He has met Mollie, and I thought you should know.'

'Well, I'm happy for you, Mona. I like the name; it's unusual. Is it serious?'

'Yes, I would say so, but I will do nothing in a hurry. That is a problem because he wants to take things forward faster. He knows his own mind, and that's the way he feels. Of course, if I moved, Mollie would go with me. How do you feel about that?'

'Well, as long as I have my regular visits, I expect it will be fine. There are always holidays as well. I'll meet him soon, I hope. Actually, I have something to tell you. I've met someone, too. Her name's Rosa, she's older than me, been married, but her husband died. No children either, which makes things easier all around.'

'I'm pleased for you, Malcolm. I think this calls for a celebration. What have you got in that fridge of yours?'

'You know me, Mona, always have a decent bottle of wine ready for such an occasion. Let's toast the future.'

When Mona came home, Mollie and Leona were watching a wildlife documentary.

'Mummy, where have you been? We've saved supper for you; it's in the oven.'

'I've been to see your Dad, Mollie, and we had an enjoyable time. He made me a meal, but I can save the one you made for me and have it tomorrow.'

'That's nice, Mummy, we're watching a great program. It's all about kangaroos; they live in families called mobs. The babies are called joeys, and they live in their mummies pouch.'

'I'll put Mollie to bed after the program. You look tired.'

'Thanks, Leona.'

Mona was asleep when Leona came back down. She woke her gently.

'Oh dear, I think I had one too many glasses of wine. Still, it was nice to see Malcolm. He's met someone: Rosa. I couldn't make him happy, and he deserves a second chance.'

'Did you tell him about Darnley?'

'I did, and he would like to meet him; he's bound to be concerned about Mollie's future. Rosa is a widow without children. So, a pretty straightforward situation. Oh dear, I feel frightened suddenly. What shall I do?'

Leona took Mona's hand. 'For the present, don't worry. You talk to Darnley and make your situation quite clear. You want to be with him, but you won't be rushed into marriage or to live with him. If he is the man I think he is, he will understand and give you the time and space that you need.'

'Dear Leona. What will I do when I can no longer sit here in the evening and tell you all my troubles and thoughts? We will be reduced to phone calls and visits.'

'You will cope and learn to talk to Darnley instead. That's how it should be, my dear. I will be here for you, and you can visit whenever you want. Don't forget the old-fashioned letter; that's something so many people have lost, and it's a pity. I will write to you, and you will write back.'

'That's what we will do, Leona. Will you make me one of your bedtime herbal drinks, please?'

'Of course. I'll be back in three minutes.'

Mona turned her head towards the window. It was still warm, but the seasons were changing. How cosy and comfortable she felt here. Why must everything change? Then, there was the fear — always the fear.

CHAPTER TWENTY SIX

'Got you, you little bastard. I've been waiting a long time for this. Not as careful as you were, are you?'

Ethan struggled to get free, but Bates was too strong.

'Get off me, Bates. You're hurting my arm.'

'Don't worry, I won't break it. It will be painful for a few days, though. It might teach you a lesson not to come here again, spying and interfering with my work. Where's your partner, by the way? Oh yes, he's too busy with his woman and baby to bother with you anymore. Things don't remain a secret for long. Dirty old bugger, what does she see in him? I envy him, though.'

'I'll tell you what she sees in Dulap, Bates. He's everything you're not. He's a decent man, considerate of others. More than that, he doesn't kill birds. Let me go, you big bully.'

In answer to that plea, Bates gave an extra tug on Ethan's arm, making him cry out with pain.

'Mr Bates, to you, sonny. By the way, there seem to be a few items missing, which belong to me.'

'The wire traps, you mean? I gave them to Dulap. He'll know what to do with them.'

Suddenly, Bates went flying. Ethan fell to the ground; his arm hurt, but he was free. Someone had hold of the gamekeeper, and whoever it was must be strong, as Ethan watched Bates being forcefully bundled off the moor and out onto the road, where he was punched to the ground.

The boy took off, amazed at what he had seen. Running all the way to Dulap's cottage, he banged on the door. Imogen answered.

'Ethan, how nice to see you. If you want Dulap, I'm afraid he's not here at the moment, and I'm not sure how long he'll be. Please come in and wait. We haven't had the chance to get to know one another very well.'

'Yes, I need to see him. Do you know where he's gone?'

'No, but he said something about collecting some pots for me so that I can plant Spring bulbs. I do this every Autumn, and I've already ordered potting compost. Sit down, Ethan. Let me get you a drink. I like hot chocolate at this time of day. How about you?'

'Yes, please, I'd like that, Imogen.'

As they settled down with their drinks, Imogen asked about his family.

'You live on a farm, don't you? Your father keeps sheep. Your family hasn't always lived there, though. A bit like me, really.'

'That's right,' Ethan answered, 'my father changed careers, which he called a mid-life crisis. My mother thought he was crazy because he knew next to nothing about farming. None of us thought he would succeed, but despite everything, he has. Mind you, he couldn't have done it without help from Jack Field, a neighbouring farmer, and also my sister, Mattie. She used to take a genuine interest in the farm, but she has other interests now. I don't know whether Dulap's told you, but my mother, Susan, started an affair with Jack. To be honest, the marriage was all but over, anyway. Still, it caused a lot of trouble and unhappiness, especially for my father, Peter. He's getting over it now, but Mum left and lives with Jack. I like Jack, always have, so there's no point in holding a grudge, is there?'

'No, there isn't, Ethan. No point at all. I left my husband, Samuel. He was the vicar here, but now his future is uncertain. He didn't take me leaving well; in fact it has made him unable to cope with his life. I have been assured that, with enough medical help, he will get better. Iris is waking up, here we go, meet Dulap's daughter.'

When Dulap returned, he found Ethan and Imogen laughing and talking and playing with the baby.

'Hey, Ethan, what a lovely surprise. Sorry, I wasn't home when you came. Went to get some pots for Imogen from Sam Wood; he's good for anything to do with gardening. Imogen loves her spring bulbs, especially Iris, hence the baby's name. Been here long?'

'A while, but that's fine. Having a great time with Imogen and Iris. She's a lovely baby, Dulap. You're very lucky, and well deserved too. Have you been anywhere else this morning?'

'No, just to get the pots, but I always stay a while with Sam. He's a nice old guy; I get vegetables from him as well. I think he's lonely and needs company. Stay and eat with us. We'll have a late breakfast or an early lunch, whichever way you see it.'

Dulap was pleased that the two of them were getting on so well and knew that his friendship with Ethan would not change that much. He picked up Iris, kissing her.

'Hello, my beauty. How's my pretty girl today? I love you so much. I believe that might have been a little smile and look at those dimples. Would you like to hold her, Ethan? Just support her head with your arm.'

Ethan sat down with the baby. She was so small and soft. She looked at him with her blue eyes as though studying him. Ethan decided that, whatever happened, he would protect her as though she was his own.

When Ethan left, Dulap walked down the path with him.

'There's something on your mind, lad. Care to tell me what it is?'

'I didn't want to say anything in front of Imogen, but Bates found me this morning, the first time he has ever crept up on me. He forced my arm behind my back. It's not so bad now; painful when I held Iris, but it was worth it.'

'What happened then?'

'Well, suddenly, Bates let go, and I found myself on my back. I watched while he was being forced off the moor, punched and left by his range rover. Whoever it was, he was dressed all in black and strong enough to get the better of Bates. I couldn't believe it.'

'Well, I'm glad you're not really hurt, Ethan. Best to stay off the moors for a while. Wait until I can go with you. Maybe at the weekend?'

Ethan made his way home, hands in his pockets, thinking about Dulap's reaction to his news. He didn't seem particularly surprised by what had happened. He was a powerful man, despite his age, having spent his life doing manual work, much of it lifting heavy equipment, building walls and sheds, repairing outhouses and boundaries. Although he was slight and wiry, that hid his strength and resilience. He could tackle Bates, but was it him?

Elsewhere, the gamekeeper nursed the bruises to his face and hands, and his painful stomach. Sipping a large whisky, he was slowly coming to terms with the attack. Who the hell was it? Dulap? He'd had run-ins with him before, but nothing you would call violent. No reporting this to the police or his employers, there was no point. He poured himself another drink. What was he to do now? For the first time in his life, he felt utterly defeated, beaten down, unable to think clearly. His attacker was fearless. If this came out, he would be a laughingstock at work and in the village. He'd been elated, catching Ethan for the first time. What luck, only to be driven off the moors, knocked down and punched. He would never feel safe again.

After the third drink, Bates lay down and slept. He'd take time off work, keep to himself and think about what to do next. If the truth came out, it would be impossible to bear. No, if that happened, he would have to leave or go on long-term sickness, with depression and stress.

The next morning, he sent a message to Hugh Curtis, explaining that he was feeling unwell and would like to take the time owing to him, apologising for the short notice. He'd be in touch in due course. The manager was surprised and a little concerned. This was not like Bates. What was going on with his head-keeper? He called around late in the afternoon.

'Roger, Just wanted to know how you are?' He was well aware Bates had been drinking heavily.

The visit annoyed Bates but tolerated the intrusion, staggering onto his feet to greet his visitor.

'I think I've been overdoing things, so a break would do me good.'

'I see. You look as though you've been in a fight. What's been happening, Roger? It's obvious that you're in pain.'

'It's nothing. I just want to be left alone, that's all.' He wanted Hugh to go. He sat down on the sofa, clutching his stomach.

'Look,' he continued, 'I'll tell you, but I don't want it to go any further. You must promise me.'

'Right, if that's what you want, but tell me.'

Bates sighed. 'Yesterday, I caught that lad, Ethan, on the moor. It's the first time I've been able to catch him. I just caught his arm and was going to escort him to the road, warning him to stay away in the future, when I was attacked myself. Whoever it was came from nowhere, and he was bloody strong. I had to drop the boy while I was bundled off the moor, punched and knocked down. I can tell you, I was frightened.'

'You do not know who this person was?'

Bates shook his head. 'Not a clue. He was all in black, with some kind of mask. It could be Dulap Whottle, but I don't know. To be honest, while this madman's about, I don't feel safe.'

'Right, take as much time as you need, and don't worry, I won't tell anyone. Keep in touch, and let me know how you are getting on. Let's hope this is the end of the affair. I'll make some excuses for the owners. Rest, get better and, Roger, watch your drinking. If you need anything, ring me.'

CHAPTER TWENTY SEVEN

October brought misty mornings, which brightened into days that were perfectly still, with slight haziness, softening the landscape. Warm days caused butterflies and bees to fly once more, while the flowering ivy was covered in blue- bottles and drone flies. Lanes were strewn with the harvest of beech mast, acorns and horse chestnut, tempting squirrels from the safety of the trees. Bird cherry produced masses of bright-red berries amongst the yellow leaves of birch and hazel. Some birds still sang, like the chaffinch and wood pigeon. Even the skylark flew up, but with a shorter flight, while pheasants dusted themselves on the warm bank sides, looking for acorns undercover.

Some nights brought high winds and storms. Then the song thrush sang its repeated notes high in a tree. Woodcock nestled in favourite spots near the woodland edge, with the wonderful spectacle of rooks as they tumbled and twisted in the gusts of wind.

Now, in copses and spinnies, seasonal fungi appeared, like the white agarics, producing delicate flowers balanced on slender stalks, gathered around the hazel stools. Most birds had gone, but those which stayed adjusted to a new life, many moving from woods to country lanes, visiting feeders and bird baths, or feeding in the fields with redwings, having left their breeding grounds in the north for an English winter.

Somehow, word had spread of the attack on Bates; people remembered the first one, and there was much speculation on who the masked stranger could be. Ethan had told Susan and Jack about it after he had been to see Dulap and Imogen.

'I can hardly believe it,' Susan remarked, 'anyway, he won't get any sympathy from us. Is your arm all right, Ethan?'

'It hurts a bit, but it's worth it to see Bates being manhandled off the moor, and he couldn't do a thing about it. What do you think, Jack?'

'Same as everyone else, I expect. He had it coming to him. Now, he is no longer the big man he thought he was.'

A few days later, Bates visited "The Curlew", only to be greeted by laughter and comments.

'Met any strangers lately, Mr Bates?' a regular asked him.

The gamekeeper scowled, bought his beer and sat well away from the bar. After one drink, he left the pub. He owed a call to Hugh Curtis because he wasn't planning to go back to work for a while. He had a sick note from the doctor, citing stress and depression, which would cover him for four weeks. Glad to be home, Bates sat in his garden, a piece of land given over to bindweed and clumps of grass and little else. He watched a flock of starlings, manoeuvring and twisting like a smoke cloud, wheeling like one bird, changing in a second from a closed formation to an extended line, then drooping suddenly like a stone onto a favourite tree where they would roost.

After years of working outside, he knew instinctively that a storm was coming. Rarely lonely, being used to his own company, now he felt very isolated. The winter might be tough this year. He checked his phone. One missed call from Hugh, asking if a visit was convenient. Nothing important, just keeping in touch.

Bates looked around the living room, which needed a tidy-up and a dusting. That could all wait. Anyway, best if Hugh thought he wasn't coping. His thoughts kept turning to Ethan, the boy who had dogged him ever since he had moved to the district, trespassing, spying and making a general nuisance of himself. Then, just as he had caught him for the first time, the little bastard had been rescued, and he didn't know who had attacked him. Well, there would be a reckoning. But how? He'd find a way without getting himself into trouble. As the day went by, Bates drank heavily, whiskey being his preferred choice, and he became increasingly angry until his hatred of Ethan took possession of his mind. Having no precise plan of how to rid himself of the boy, he decided the place to start would be the farm. Each day, he parked his land rover near, but not outside the entrance, so that he had a clear view of who came and went. Ethan left home early, and Bates thought that was his best chance.

It wasn't until the third day of his surveillance that Ethan strolled out, making his way to visit Susan. Slowly, keeping his distance, Bates followed, surprised when his victim didn't appear to be going to see Dulap or to the moor. Jack Field's farm. Why was he going there? Any gossip about Susan's change of address had never reached Bates. He waited until Ethan came out.

Two hours later, Ethan made an appearance, turning right without a coherent plan of where to go next. Deciding to give the moor a miss, he'd head for the woods instead, the same woods where Leona had her vision. Turning left, briskly walking on the wide dirt path, and unaware that Bates was parking up to follow him on foot. The path was a long one, at the end of which Ethan had a choice of going left, right or straight on. Bates followed as closely and silently as he could. However, the four large tumblers of whiskey and the beer had muddled his senses, making him unsteady on his legs and clumsy. Ethan heard breaking twigs, and, spinning around, he saw an enraged and drunk gamekeeper. Instead of going deeper into the woods, Ethan took the right fork along a very narrow, overgrown path, pointing to the fact that few people came this way. He knew exactly where this would take him, hoping he could shake off his pursuer. Overgrown brambles and giant stinging nettles tore and stung his legs and hands as he made his way as quickly as possible.

Not long now, he could almost smell his way to the foreboding, dank stretch of water known as "Hedder's Pond", a small lake, always covered in mist, with a strange and almost evil atmosphere. Its depth was unknown, but certainly deep. Devoid of wildlife, for no birds nested here or swam on its surface, it remained a strange, murky place. The margins of the pond were deceptive, for they were a tangle of weeds and mud. Ethan had come upon the place months ago and knew it well. He had discovered a way across the water, just a little way from the edge, where it was safe to cross because of a deposit of bricks and rubble just below the surface.

Bates stumbled into view, drunk and out of control. He followed Ethan across the water, where he thought it was safe, but his mind wasn't functioning, his vision blurred and heavy footsteps made his way difficult. He lost his footing, falling into deep water and thick, oozy mud. Swearing, he tried to reach the pond's edge, clutching blindly onto the reeds. Ethan watched in horror as Bates sank further down; then he fled. He wanted to get home, see Peter and Mattie, and never, ever come to this place again. Maybe Bates would get out, maybe not, but he would tell no one what had happened that day.

It was two weeks before the body of the gamekeeper was found. When Bates failed to contact Hugh Curtis, he asked the police to find out if he was at home. Curtis told them he was fearful because of the man's state of mind and his drinking. Empty bottles of whiskey were discarded in nearly every room, but there was no sign of Bates; no one had any idea where he could be. A search was launched, using dogs, starting on the moors and then the surrounding countryside. There was no trace of him. His ex-wife was contacted, but 'no, she hadn't seen him and didn't want to either.'

Rumours and speculation were rife, especially in "The Curlew", with everyone having a view about what might have happened. No one volunteered to help the police find him.

Then, someone spotted a land rover, half hidden in woods, about half a mile from the road, obviously parked there when driving further had been impossible. Eventually, the search led to "Hedder's Pond" and the grim discovery of his body. There was no reason to believe anyone else was involved in the death, although the police couldn't explain why Bates would have gone there. The coroner gave his verdict as 'death by misadventure', noting that the body contained large amounts of alcohol.

The funeral was a lonely affair, attended by Hugh Curtis and his wife, other gamekeepers and a representative from the estate. However, the rumours didn't end with the death. Why would Bates go near "Hedder's Pond"? Dulap was puzzled too, but, knowing Bates as he did, he worked out a reason, especially coming so soon after the humiliation of his attack. Maybe he was chasing someone, his temper, as always, getting the better of him, fuelled by drink.

Dulap saw Ethan and tested his theory.

'I'm just going to the farm to see Ethan, Imogen. I'll see how Peter is too; maybe he needs help on the farm.'

'O.k. See you later.'

Peter was pleased to see his friend. 'Hi, Dulap, let's go in for a bit. It's been ages.'

The kitchen was inviting and warm. Mattie was there, but not Ethan.

'How's it going,' Peter asked. 'What's it like having a baby in the cottage? I'm thrilled for you. You're a lucky man.'

'I am, Peter. Falling in love and becoming a father at my age. Can you believe it? Is Ethan about?'

'He's in his room if you want to go up.'

'I think there's something wrong with him, Dulap,' Mattie remarked, 'he seems to be really down.'

Dulap knocked on Ethan's door. 'Ethan, it's Dulap. Can I come in, lad?'

'Yes, the door's unlocked.'

'Hello, I've been wondering why I haven't seen you lately. You've heard about Bates, I suppose?'

'Yes, of course I have. It's no concern of mine, Dulap. He won't be missed by anyone.'

'Strange that he ended up in Hedder's Pond, though, don't you think?'

'No idea. Have you seen Dad and Mattie?'

'Ethan, are you hiding something? You seem strange. Whatever you tell me will be our secret, you know that.'

'I know nothing. Leave me alone! Why should I know anything? Bates was an evil man who got into trouble and drowned.'

Dulap would not let this drop until he got the truth.

'You're a distressed lad and frightened, too. I can help you, but you must talk to me. I'm the only one you can confide in about this.'

'Nothing, Dulap. I...I saw him drowning. He was chasing me. He was in such a rage...I had to get away, but I didn't touch him. If he'd got hold of me?'...

'He would have battered you, Ethan. You could have been the one who drowned. Bates died because he couldn't control his temper, drank too much and was trying to take revenge on an innocent person. You have nothing to feel guilty about. Only you and I know the truth, and that dies with Bates. Now, I'll go downstairs, and you come down soon.'

Ethan flung his arms around Dulap and let a flow of tears release themselves.

'Thank you, Dulap. I've been so frightened, thinking the police might come round any time...'

'It's all over, Ethan. You can move on now. Everything's fine.'

CHAPTER TWENTY EIGHT

Mona was satisfied with her life. She didn't mind travelling between home and Lincolnshire as long as she could continue to see Darnley. Living with Mollie and Leona, she had no intention of giving it all up soon. Hoping he would understand her feelings, she looked forward to many happy times. However, Leona didn't share this optimism. She had met Darnley once and liked him immensely. His presence filled the room; he was friendly and caring, and his love for Mona was touching. He had many qualities, but patience was not one of them. She foresaw trouble between them unless a compromise could be reached on when the relationship would move forward.

It was the middle of November, and rain had been persistent for over a week, looking set to continue.

Mollie came into the sitting room with a new jigsaw.

'Hello, dear. Going to start your jigsaw? What's the picture?'

'Yes, Mummy got it for me from a charity shop. The women said that someone completes them to make sure the pieces are all there. Do you think they do, Leona? It's a country scene, with children and ducks. I like these kinds of pictures best.'

'Oh yes, so do I, Mollie. I don't know if they check them before they put them out for sale, but I think it's likely. Otherwise, no one would buy them again. It's a lovely picture. If you want any help to complete it, just ask. Seeing your Dad on Saturday?'

'No, Mummy said something about a friend coming here. She wants me to meet him. Do you know about him?'

'Well, we have met, but only once. I don't know a lot about him, but he seems nice, and your Mum is very fond of him. Do you know his name, Mollie?'

'She told me, but I've forgotten. It's a funny name. I quite liked it. Mummy will not leave us, will she, Leona? I couldn't bear that.'

'Oh, no, sweetheart, Mummy would never leave you, so don't worry about it. Maybe you should tell her about your fears sometime when you can talk privately.'

On Saturday, Darnley arrived promptly. Mona was understandably nervous, well aware of the importance of his visit and meeting with Mollie. She asked Mollie to answer the door. 'That will be Darnley. I know how much he has been looking forward to meeting you.'

'Hello,' Darnley said, 'You must be Mollie. May I come in?'

'Yes, you can if you like,' Mollie answered tentatively. She had not expected such a tall, imposing man. Dressed in a dark green suit, bow tie and cream shirt, he put Mollie at ease, waylaying any doubts she had about him. He had an unfailing knack for engaging people, especially children. A bit like a child himself, he was gentle and natural. Soon Mollie was talking to him about her life, school and interests. Mona and Leona looked on with interest and relief.

Lunch was relaxed, with Darnley insisting on doing the washing-up; the rest of the day, Darnley helped Mollie with her science homework. When he left, Mona was feeling tired but relieved. Things had gone better than expected, and when she put Mollie to bed, she talked to her about Darnley.

'I really like him, Mummy. He's funny and made me laugh, and he really helped with the homework.'

'That's nice, darling. He is a very kind man, and I love him very much. Shall we have him over at Christmas?'

'Yes...but what about Dad? Can he come, too?'

'Of course, if he wants to. I'll ask him tomorrow.'

When Malcolm came the next day to collect Mollie, Mona broached the subject.

'We were all wondering if you could join us for Christmas day? Bring your friend as well.'

His reply took Mona by surprise. 'My friend, as you call her, has decided that the relationship isn't working, and she's finished it. I thought everything was going well. So, you want me to come around and play happy families, do you? No doubt this Darnley will be here?'

'I'm so sorry, Malcolm, I did not know. I can see how bitter you are. If you don't come over, what will you do?'

'Go to my parents, what else?'

'Can't you come, for Mollie's sake? She will be so disappointed. I know, this is a setback for you, but you will meet someone else...'

Malcolm laughed. 'Tell you what, Mona. Why don't I ask Leona for a reading, only I might not like the results. Is Mollie ready?'

'Yes, she's just coming.'

After Mona had seen them away, she joined Leona in the sitting room, who looked up from her book. 'Well, my dear, I don't need to be a clairvoyant to know something's wrong. I could hear crosswords from Malcolm.'

'Here's your tea, Leona. No tea bags, made from loose tea, just as you like it.' Mona sighed. 'I asked him to spend Christmas day here, but his girlfriend, Rosa, has broken up with him, and he's unhappy about it. I suppose if Darnley weren't coming it would be different, but, of course, he must come. Maybe Malcolm will change his mind; I do hope so.'

A similar conversation was taking place between Susan and Peter. She wanted Jack and herself to come to the farm to celebrate Christmas, but Peter wasn't sure about it.

'I accept your relationship with Jack now, but as for having him here? Well, that's a different matter. Just not sure I'm ready, Susan.'

'I thought,' Susan replied, 'that we could ask Dulap and Imogen as well. It would be lovely to have a baby in the house, too. Still, I understand, Peter. You liked Jack once...you were good friends.'

'Sure, some friend he turned out to be. Tell you what, Susan, I hear what you say, let me think about it. I know Ethan and Mattie would like him to come, although they see him all the time. Don't suppose you fancy a walk to "The Curlew", do you? I've no pressing work this afternoon.'

Familiar faces were glad to see them, including Dulap, who came and joined them.

'Glad to see both of you and that you're still friends, despite everything.'

'Thanks, Dulap,' Peter answered, 'nice to see you, too. We wanted to ask if you all wanted to come to us on Christmas day?'

'Sure, sounds good to me. Imogen will be pleased. She doesn't have many friends, and, although she keeps it to herself, she needs company.'

'That's settled then,' Susan said.

'Will you and Jack be coming?'

Susan looked at Peter. 'That's a moot point at the moment. I want everyone to be there, but it's up to Peter.'

'Looks as though I'm outnumbered then, doesn't it? Yes, Jack can come, but I can't promise to be best buddies anymore, though there will be no unpleasantness, I can assure you.'

Susan smiled. 'Thanks, Peter. By the way, Dulap, what do you think of Bates drowning? No one seemed to know why he was there.

The police can't understand it. It's strange. Still, I didn't like the man and made no secret of it. I used to worry about Ethan walking on the moors.'

This was a topic that Dulap didn't want to discuss. 'Another drink, anyone.'

Dulap came back with the drinks, and Susan started another topic.

'I hope you don't mind me asking about the vicar. I just wondered how he was doing?'

'Don't mind at all, Susan. He's been admitted to hospital. Imogen is in touch with the doctor about his condition and treatment. He seems to have suffered a complete mental breakdown. He talks about her, but never about Iris, it could be he doesn't remember her. Imogen wants to see him, but they don't recommend this for the present. Of course, he will need a lot of recovery time, even when he comes out. There's talk of him going to live with his sister, Marie, and her husband, Dennis. They have two girls.'

Susan and Peter strolled back. When they got to Jack's farm, they hugged and said their 'goodbyes.' Somehow, a settlement had been reached, an understanding between them and a closure to years of unhappy living.

Samuel was having his weekly session with Mr Ruskin, his psychiatrist.

'Sit down on the easy chair, Samuel. You look much better. How do you feel?'

'Feel?...in what way, feel?...'

'Well, I mean, in yourself. You haven't been well, you know, but I think you are making excellent progress. What would you like to talk about? The last time we met, you told me about your study and how you liked to work there.'

'Oh, did I? Where was that?'

'It was when you lived in the vicarage. You became unhappy, and that's when we stepped in to help you.'

'Did you? That's nice.'

Mr Ruskin laughed. 'You're very welcome, Samuel. The medication is helping, too. It can take a while to get the right combination, but I am very pleased with your progress.'

Samuel looked puzzled. 'Where is she?'

'Who, Samuel?'

'I think she lived with me? I remember her being there...with me.'

Dr Ruskin changed the conversation. 'Do you remember your sister, Marie, and her husband, Dennis? They are coming to see you tomorrow.'

'Coming to see me? What about her? Imogen?'

'Of course, you will see her as well, but not tomorrow. She asks all the time about you though. What would you say about going to live with your sister for a while? They live in Whitby, near the sea. Do you remember going there?'

Samuel's eyes became bright. 'The sea...oh yes...I like the sea. Can I go now?'

Mr Ruskin smiled. 'Of course, you can, soon. They have a room, all ready for you. You can go back with them tomorrow.'

Mr Ruskin had thought long and hard about Samuel's case. His assessment was that he would never fully recover, but with help, he could lead a relatively normal life. Samuel's world hovered between reality and fantasy. He remembered Imogen, but little about his life with her at the vicarage. Sometimes, he referred to her as an angel. Unfortunately, there was no way to predict his reaction if he saw her, and this troubled the doctor. There would be strict conditions over his patient's stay at Whitby; Samuel must never be left alone, especially outside, and he must have his medicine without fail. Certain objects were to be moved out of his reach, such as knives, belts, etc. As to the long-term? Well, that remained to be seen.

CHAPTER TWENTY NINE

Dulap was bathing Iris, a job he really liked. At nearly five months old, she was a happy baby, delighting in the feel of the warm water and the soft bubbles.

'Right, my precious, let's get you wrapped in the towel and find Mummy.'

Imogen had just finished speaking to Mr Ruskin. While Dulap dried and dressed Iris, she told him about the call.

'Did I tell you Samuel has a sister, Marie? She's married with two daughters. Mr Ruskin thinks he's well enough to leave the hospital and live with them; see how it goes. So, he's going to Whitby tomorrow. Marie doesn't work, so there will always be someone with him in the house and also when he goes out. I don't really want to see him, so I was relieved when the doctor said it would be unwise for me to do so.'

'He's probably right, my love,' Dulap reflected. 'I've been shocked by how ill Samuel has been. This change seems to be a good idea.'

'Yes, Samuel was never a healthy man, Dulap. He took everything so much to heart and found problems even when there weren't any. I admit I was totally unsuitable to be a vicar's wife and the distressing arguments it caused. I'm not sure what I would have done if I hadn't met you. Then there was all the baby business.'

Dulap put Iris into her baby chair, so she was safe and could see them. He hugged Imogen. 'I know it's hard, but never blame yourself.

People make unsuitable unions all the time. I was just glad I was here for you. I've never been so happy.'

When Marie and Dennis arrived at the hospital, Mr Ruskin greeted them and ushered them into his office.

'Please sit down. Before you see Samuel, I wanted to tell you what to expect. When he first came to us, he was threatening suicide. Who knows if he would have done so, if not helped by a friend from the church, and given into our care. I understand his troubles started because of his wife leaving him, although I believe he has never been strong mentally. He has responded well to counselling, and his medication is crucial to his progress. I will supply you with all the information you need and give you a month's supply of medicine. I have written to your practice in Whitby, and you need to make sure he's registered with them. Contact me if there are problems. Now, time to meet Samuel. Don't expect too much. He's still somewhat confused about what's happened to him, but he will know you both, so no worries there.'

'Has Imogen seen him?' Marie asked.

'No, he didn't ask to at first, but he has done recently and refers to her as his wife. However, he also refers to her as an angel, as though Imogen is some mystical being. I would like you to keep a record of his behaviour, and anything that seems relevant to you. It all helps with his recovery. Now, I'll take you to a private room where you can meet him.'

On entering, they found Samuel sitting quietly. He didn't seem to know who they were at first, but then he smiled and rose to greet them.

'Hello, Samuel,' Dennis said.

'Yes...yes, of course, Marie and Dennis. How nice to see you. Are you staying?'

'No,' Marie answered, 'we would like you to come and stay with us instead; there's a room all ready for you, and the girls are looking forward to seeing you. Remember them? Daisy and Violet.'

'Just like two flowers,' Samuel mused. 'Daisy...Violet. Have I met them before?'

'Oh yes, many times. Shall we go back today?'

Samuel looked alarmed. 'Does the doctor know?'

Mr Ruskin walked forward and said, 'I know all about it, and the change will do you good. I'm told you you like the sea. You can go there and paddle in it and look in rock pools with the girls. I'm told you love to do that.'

Samuel readily agreed to go. He enjoyed looking out of the window, in the car, then fell asleep for most of the journey. When he woke up, he smelt it...sensed it...the salty, foamy expanse of the sea. He longed to see it, but they went straight home to a three-bedroomed bungalow, which Samuel said he remembered and had visited many times before. Daisy and Violet were genuinely pleased to see their uncle. They were fourteen and fifteen, respectively.

'Hello, uncle, we're so glad you've come. Everything's ready for you.'

Samuel smiled. 'Oh yes…pleased to see you too. Are you Daisy?'

'No, I'm Violet. We have lots of things planned. Only if you want to, of course.'

'Thank you…thank you. Can I go to the sea?'

'Of course, you can,' Marie said, 'plenty of time for that. The sea is wild at the moment; winter winds, you see. Let's all sit down, and I'll make tea. Violet made a special cake, coconut and jam sponge.'

Samuel ate his cake with relish and drank three cups of tea. He appeared happy and relaxed. 'May I have a sleep now, please?'

'Of course, you can, Samuel,' his sister said, 'I'll show you to your room, come and go as you want. There are a few rules here, but let me know if you want anything. I expect you are tired after the journey. I have medication for you from Mr Ruskin. Those may have made you tired.'

'Do I see him later?'

Marie smiled. 'No, you are having a long holiday with us, but he will phone, and you can talk to him then. Now, have a good rest. Supper will be in a couple of hours.' Marie left the door slightly open when she left.

'Everything all right?' Dennis asked.

'Yes, I think so. He may sleep. We need to give him privacy but monitor him, too. One thing worries me a bit: his fascination with the sea. He must never go out on his own.' Marie felt an unease, which she couldn't shift, but she was determined to do all she could to help her brother. Tomorrow, they would walk by the sea together.

When Samuel joined the family for supper, refreshed from his sleep, he wanted to chat.

'A lovely meal. Delicious. Where did I live before?'

'You mean the hospital, Samuel?' Marie asked.

'Yes...was it. I like it better here. Will I go back there?'

'We all hope not,' Dennis answered.

'Can I go to the sea? Will it be calm or stormy? I like calm best.'

'Yes, we can all go tomorrow; we'll have a walk around the town first, have something to eat, then a visit to the sea.'

The next day found them wandering around the town. It wasn't too busy, which was just as well because Samuel had an aversion to crowds. He kept close to the family, and, deciding to skip the meal, they headed down to the beach. The winds had died down, and the sea was fairly calm, its vast expanse stretching into the distance. Suddenly, flocks of herring gulls and a few common gulls rose, flying away from the human visitors. Pieces of seaweed floated near the edge, and the girls skipped ahead, stopping to pick up shells.

Samuel stopped walking and stood looking at the ocean, not at anything in particular, but mumbling to himself. Marie told the girls not to go too far, and then went to stand next to her brother, trying to catch his words. He turned round at her approach, and Marie gently took hold of his arm.

'Do you remember when Dennis and I moved to Whitby, before the girls were born? Do you remember that?'

Samuel turned to face the sea again. Speaking as to himself, he said, 'I can't see her...out there. Where is she? I thought if I came, she would wait for me...I see her sometimes...like an angel. I want to go back home now...have tea and cake...like yesterday.'

'Of course, Samuel, let's do that. It's cold, and it's raining. Take my hand. We'll soon be back.'

Later, Marie took Dennis to one side while Daisy and Violet kept Samuel company.

'I saw you talking to him and thought it was best to keep away.'

'Yes, I couldn't catch everything he said, but I know he was thinking about Imogen. He called her an angel and expected to see her. Maybe he thinks she comes from the sea. I don't know. We'll record it in the notes for the doctor. Still, he seems happy enough now we are home, and he gets on well with the girls. Maybe we should limit our visits to the sea if it upsets him. I thought this afternoon I'll get him involved with putting up the Christmas tree and decorating it, giving him something to occupy his mind. Mum and Dad want to come for Christmas. They visited him at the hospital, but it would be lovely for us all to be together. Oh, Dennis, why did this have to happen? Why did Imogen have to leave like that? Who's this man she's with, anyway? I suppose, the baby is his, not Samuel's? What a mess.'

Dennis gave her a hug. 'Hey, it will be fine; try not to worry too much. Let's have a great Christmas. In answer to your question about the baby, I'm sure it's not Samuel's. He never talks about her, does he?'

'No, he doesn't. It's best that way, and she should never be mentioned. Goodness knows how he might re-act.'

'Agreed, Marie. Absolutely.'

CHAPTER THIRTY

'Are you ready, Jack?'

Jack didn't answer, looking out on a cold, drizzly Christmas morning. Concerned about how Peter would react to him, he remembered how good the friendship had been, working together, talking and laughing; he had enjoyed his time with Peter. Just one year ago, Susan still lived at the farm; a lot had happened since then. Now, Susan shared his life, and he loved waking up each morning by her side, no longer a lonely man, but it had cost him dear. His mind wandered to "Hedder's Pond", a place he had not seen for years. Lonely and forbidding, he knew about the superstition connected with the place. Still, he wanted to go there so he could see where Bates had drowned and derive some satisfaction that the brute was gone forever. He planned a visit in the New Year.

'Jack, did you hear me? It's time to go.'

'Oh, sorry, Susan. I was just thinking and didn't hear you. I'm ready.'

'Don't worry about Peter. He might be cold towards you at first, and you won't become best friends overnight, but after a few glasses of wine, he'll thaw. He'll deal with it in his own time. Got everything? Presents? Bottles? Let's go then.'

When they arrived, Dulap and Imogen were already there. She was helping Mattie prepare the vegetables, while Dulap was occupied with Iris, helped by Ethan, fascinated with the baby. He loved to watch her, listening to all her noises and chuckles, even changing her nappy and dressing her.

'Hello, everyone,' Jack called out. Peter greeted them, taking their coats and packages. 'Come in. Help yourself to a drink.' He offered a hand to Jack, which was gratefully accepted.

'Despite everything, Jack, it's good to see you both. I want to make this a proper family Christmas.'

'Thanks, Peter,' Jack replied, 'I really appreciate it. Can we help with preparations?'

'No, but tell you what, Jack. Maybe we can take a stroll around the farm later. What do you say?'

Jack smiled. 'I couldn't think of anything I'd rather do.'

At about the same time, Mona welcomed Darnley into the house. Even though Malcolm would not be joining them, Mollie was pleased to see the guest, having taken an immediate liking to him. She gave him a hug, her small hands barely stretching around his ample stomach. Wearing a multi-coloured Christmas jumper over green cord trousers, he swooped up the girl's small body, lifting her into the air, saying, 'Happy Christmas, Mollie, we are going to have a wonderful day. I expect my waist-line will increase by the end of it all.' Mollie insisted on sitting next to the big man, much to the delight of Mona and Leona.

Later on, while the presents were opened, they drank Bailey's and ate mince pies. Darnley gave Mollie a pair of china skating dolls, one boy, one girl, dressed in red velvet with a white border and a pair of skates in each of their hands. She also got a soil sampling kit and a rain measuring gauge. Leona was presented with a beautifully embroidered shawl to replace the old woollen one she always wore and a bottle of her favourite liquor. Darnley was rather secretive about his present for Mona. She was pleased with her new laptop...and a ring...a simple gold design with opals and a garnet. 'No pressure, Mona. I wanted you to have it.'

Mona and Leona retired into the kitchen to wash up.

'Well, that was a surprise, my dear. A lovely ring, not too fussy, perfect. How do you feel about it?'

'It's a beautiful ring. Of course, it is an engagement present, and I intend to marry him. I kept hoping that Malcolm might come for Mollie's sake. I do hope he went to his parents, so he's not alone. It was probably for the best, though, with Mollie getting on so well with Darnley and then the ring. I can imagine him sitting at the table, sullen and angry. Still, I feel bad about the situation.'

'You're right, my dear. Anyway, he'll be collecting Mollie tomorrow and having some quality time with his daughter. Will Darnley be here when he comes?'

'Yes, he will. I'll handle it as best I can and make sure that Mollie is ready to go. Other than that, maybe it's best that he meets Darnley because he will be a part of Molly's life.'

At Whitby, everyone was busy preparing for a later Christmas meal, cooking, laying the table and making the bungalow look festive.

Samuel and Marie's parents had just arrived, very pleased to see their son looking happy, his intense blue eyes gaining some of their brightness. Mary and Tom were eager to talk to Marie and Daniel with an update on his progress, but that would have to wait. The meal was nearly ready, to be served on the best china plates, with wine from crystal glasses.

After the main course, there was an interval before pudding was served.

'It's really lovely to be with you all,' Mary said.

'No...not everyone,' Samuel replied,... 'someone is not here...where is she?... the one who lived with me.' He started to cry.

'Don't be sad, uncle,' Violet said, 'cry if you want to; it will make you feel better. She hasn't gone, and I'm sure you will see her again.'

'Yes...yes...I will see her. I'm cold...so cold.'

Marie fetched a throw to put over his shoulders. 'There, Samuel, you'll be warmer soon. How about some Christmas pudding and custard? Same for everyone? There's pavlova too.'

After lunch, Samuel went to his bedroom for a rest.

'He always has a nap at this time,' explained Daniel. 'He's taking antidepressants and other medicine, which make him sleepy. Let's all sit down; the washing-up can wait. I'll make some tea, and we might talk about how we can best help Samuel.'

Marie started the conversation. 'Most of the time, Samuel is quiet and like his former self. The doctor at the hospital, Mr Ruskin, was very approachable and kept us informed about Samuel's progress, especially if there were any changes. As you know, he had threatened suicide before being taken into care. The staff there really looked after him well, and he seemed to improve. However, as you saw during the meal, he is still very confused. Imogen leaving him tipped him over the edge when he was feeling unhappy and vulnerable.'

'I really can't forgive Imogen,' Mary said, 'how could she leave? Samuel's a kind, loving man. She had a lovely home; everything she could have wanted, didn't she?'

'Things are rarely that simple,' Marie answered, 'what Imogen wanted, more than anything, was a baby. A natural enough desire, surely? Apparently, her conversations with Mr. Ruskin revealed there were infertility problems, which Samuel was not inclined to address. Their marriage would never have lasted. Apart from other difficulties, Imogen hated her role of a vicar's wife, and, well, there is something which neither of you knows about.'

'Oh?' said Tom, 'now what?'

'Imogen met someone else, and she lives with him, and they have a baby girl, Iris.'

'When did all this happen, Marie? Why weren't we told before? I can't believe this.'

Daniel tried to calm the situation by saying, 'We know, and we apologise for not telling you sooner. This has been a difficult time for all of us. We thought, maybe wrongly, that you might have driven over there to sort things out. We thought, back then, it was best not to interfere. Imogen had gone, and Samuel needed help. That's all there is to it.'

Marie continued. 'Yes, we thought about going there ourselves because we knew, from Samuel's phone calls, that they were having problems, but we didn't know how bad things had got. Well, that's in the past, so let's all move on and focus our attention on Samuel. What we were thinking, given that we don't know what the future holds; is whether we could share caring for him. Sometimes here, and sometimes with you. The last thing any of us want is to see Samuel hospitalised again. The girls are more than happy to share a room when he is here.'

'Yes, absolutely,' Tom answered, 'we must all pull together for Samuel. We can have him stay any time, and we'll leave it to you to make the arrangements.'

It was boxing day, and at Leona's house, Malcolm was due to arrive at any moment. There was tension in the house. Darnley put his arm around Mona. 'If you want me to make myself scarce, just say. I can see this is difficult for you.'

'No, Darnley, you're part of my life now and, therefore, part of Mollie's too. I am delighted she likes you so much. You have completely won her over. Malcolm doesn't need to be jealous. We just have to give it time. I'll see if Mollie's ready.'

'I'm ready, Mummy. I don't think I've forgotten anything. How long am I staying with Daddy?'

'That's up to you both. A few days, at least. Just let me know.'

Malcolm arrived; he looked pale and tired, and his mood was subdued. Mona introduced him to Darnley, who shook his hand, showing none of his flamboyant nature but just very polite. After they had gone, Mona gave Darnley a hug. 'That went well, don't you think? Now you've met each other. Come on, let's join Leona. I feel quite exhausted but happy.'

Susan and Jack invited Dulap and Imogen for tea on Boxing Day. The women liked each other and got on so well that a strong friendship was forming. They would meet every week, alternating between the two homes. Now, life would be less lonely for them both.

A few days later, they met at the cottage. The place intrigued Susan. 'Has Dulap lived here all his life?'

'Oh, yes, he shared it with his parents until they died. When I moved in, it was cosy enough, but, I must admit, it needed sprucing up. Hence the new curtains, rugs and cover for the sofa. The nursery needed redecorating, too. Of course, there's no central heating, but we are hoping to get a grant to help with that. We have an excellent case, especially as we have a baby.'

Susan sipped her tea, saying, 'It's funny, but we've done the same thing, I mean leaving our husbands. Peter and I had long ceased to be lovers, more like good friends. We rowed a lot about the move here from our previous life; I mean, what did he know about farming?

Still, with the help of Jack and Dulap; Mattie as well in the beginning, he's made it work. I assume Dulap is the father of Iris? I hope you don't mind me asking?'

'She is, and I don't mind you asking at all. When I got pregnant and ultimately left Samuel, he reacted badly, basically stopped functioning, and I had to enlist the help of a woman who is part of the church committee. He was threatening to kill himself, and that's when the Bishop intervened. Samuel was hospitalised and put in a psychiatric ward. I wanted to see him, but his doctor, Mr Ruskin, advised against it. I have been in touch frequently, though, and kept informed about his progress. Samuel seems forgetful and bewildered by what's happened. He has a range of medications to help with his depression and to calm him. Now, he is living with his sister, Marie, and her family, Dennis and their daughters, who like him a lot. His parents are involved as well, so he has lots of support.'

'Does he know about Iris?'

'Yes, I think so, but he never mentions her, which is good, making things less complicated. Of course, he's lost his living and the vicarage. I didn't enjoy being a vicar's wife, and I should have realised that from the start. All the tea parties, jumble sales, Christmas and Easter events, and so on. I tried, but then, of course, the question of having a baby brought its own problems. We both had tests, but it didn't help. I went for walks to get away from the vicarage and found myself outside the cottage one day and met Dulap. At first, he was a friend, someone I confided in, and then we became lovers. I spent my pregnancy living at the vicarage, but not sure what to say to

Samuel. He knew the baby wasn't his; we hadn't been intimate for months. Then, after her birth, I left. All I wanted was to be with Dulap and Iris right here.'

'Wow, all this was going on, and I had no idea. If I'd known you then, I could have helped you. I'm glad things have worked out so well. My situation was less complicated, and Mattie and Ethan have adapted well to the change. After a period of anger and shock, Peter has even patched up his friendship with Jack. Do you think you will see Samuel again, Imogen?'

'I don't want to; can't see the point. There will have to be a divorce at some point, of course. I really hope that's the end for me.'

'I hope so too,' Susan replied.

CHAPTER THIRTY ONE

The start of the New Year had seen heavy rain and some flooding. Now, at the end of February, bulbs had already pushed their pretty heads towards the weakened sun. In Leona's garden, the bright blue and pink anemones were the first to brighten the many pots outside her window. Soon, the delicate crocuses and spring iris would follow. A patch of snowdrops struggled underneath the spindle tree beside the bright yellow aconites.

Leona was spending more time on her own now that Mona and Mollie were going to visit Darnley most weekends. There was a rather sensitive balancing act for Mona regarding Malcolm so that he could spend time with his daughter.

Leona herself had experienced two other changes, both of which caused her to wonder rather than to worry about. The first of these was the frequent visits by Malcolm whenever Mona and Mollie were away. Sometimes, he would sit with her in complete silence for hours, just happy in her company. At other times, he would talk while Leona just listened, content to be of service or play the role of a councillor. She was expecting him today for lunch. There was a chicken stew cooking away nicely.

The second change in her life was because of the sudden visions that had returned. She saw movements just out of sight, which vanished when she turned round. Leona expected them and suspected they might become fully visible before long.

Right now, she sat on the garden bench, which she had painted light green, in a mood of calm and reflection. It would not be too long before Mona and Mollie moved to Lincolnshire to start their new life with Darnley. How would she feel, living completely on her own again? As always, change would not be too difficult, although she knew she would miss her little family very much. But, she was used to changing, always with plans to keep her busy.

The sun was still weak, struggling to exert its power on the earth. When it found a gap in the clouds, its face shone through as though trying to show its dominance. Something flashed in front of her and the surrounding space, and with it, a sweet perfume, her mother's favourite. Next time, Leona might see her again.

Going indoors, she strolled around the kitchen, waiting for the kettle to boil. Malcolm had rung to let her know he was on his way. The doorbell sounded...

'I'm glad to see you, Malcolm. Come in out of the wind. Lunch won't be long. Any news?'

'My old cat, Maisy, died. It was very peaceful and not unexpected. I had her remains cremated and yesterday sprinkled them on the church grounds, next to some snowdrops. I shall go there often to remember her; I can't see why such places should only be for people who have died. Do you?'

'I do agree, Malcolm. It's a lovely idea. You have something else to tell me, don't you?'

Malcolm smiled. 'I do; you know what people are going to say beforehand. Like when you used to give readings.'

'I just told them the truth, as I experienced it; I made nothing up. Many of my clients went away much happier than when they came in, but occasionally, it didn't happen like that. I remember one particular woman who had had several miscarriages and was desperate to have a baby. I felt extremely uncomfortable about giving her a reading, but when I saw a baby without a face, that meant one of two outcomes: either another miscarriage or the baby would be born dead.'

'How dreadful,' Malcolm answered. 'What did you tell her?'

'Even now, the memory of that day is painful to talk about. I couldn't lie to her, so I told her what I had seen. She would eventually have a healthy baby, and she did. I sometimes see her in the village. The trouble was, at the time of the reading, she went away extremely upset. Later on, her husband came banging on my door, shouting at me but apologised sometime later. Still, I regret telling her that it was a stupid thing to do. I don't practise anymore, and my life is less stressful. Anyway, I don't have the same insight I used to have.'

Their conversation continued over lunch. Leona asked, 'What is this other news you have?'

Malcolm laughed. 'You know me too well, Leona. After my break-up, I waited a while but then gave the dating business another go. I've only known her for a few weeks, but it looks hopeful. We get on well and laugh a lot, which is always a good sign. This stew is delicious, by the way.'

'Thank you. It's always good to have someone to share a meal with. I'm very pleased to hear your news. What's her name?'

'Anna. She's been married but has no children, although I would take on someone else's. She wants children, and I'd be thrilled to be a father again. We want to be honest with each other from the start; it's early days, I know, but I have such a good feeling about this. How are Mona and Mollie getting along with Darnley? I guess things are working out. I found it all difficult at first, but I'm glad for them now. Darnley seems like a really decent man. Do they have plans to live together in Lincolnshire?'

'Yes, I would say things are heading in that direction; talk to Mona about it.'

'I will,' Malcolm replied, 'when I see her next. I'll be having Mollie next weekend so that we can discuss it then. We'll start divorce proceedings some time soon. It's strange, Leona...after scattering Maisy's ashes, I felt a release from my old life and an ability to start a new one. It was as though Maisy was telling me it was time I did. I felt her rubbing my legs like she always did; such a strange sensation. Do you think that might happen again? I'm going to that spot tomorrow.'

'You really loved your Maisy, and I think it's possible that, in some way, which we can't fully understand, she is still here with you. I have strange experiences all the time, which don't worry me, but they can take me unawares. So, when you feel Maisy, savour the experience. You will be all the richer for it. When are you seeing Anna again?'

'Tomorrow. She doesn't live too far away, about four miles. We both have cars, and this time I'm going there. So far, we've met during the day. I don't want to put any pressure on her to stay over.'

'Quite right, Malcolm, just as it should be. I'll be thinking of you.'

'I'd better be going now, Leona. You've brought some sanity into my life, and I'm so grateful to you. I'll let you know how things progress.'

'I know things will work out for you both. Come round whenever you want. I'd like to meet Anna when you're both ready.'

Leona had a last walk in the garden before the light faded. She gently touched the purple and orange blooms of the crocuses. Another shadow...she held up her hands to touch it...a dove...a divine moment...

When Malcolm arrived home, he called Anna. She would make a meal for them. She was happy...looking forward to seeing him.

Later, Mona phoned Malcolm. They would be back on Friday, and there were things she needed to discuss; also, Mollie was missing him. How was he? Had he seen Leona lately?

After the call, Mona talked to Darnley. 'Malcolm sounded fine. I was expecting him to sound a bit well...depressed, but no, he seemed upbeat and friendly. A change from a few weeks ago. It's a relief.'

'Maybe he's met someone, too. I hope so.'

CHAPTER THIRTY TWO

Early March and the lambing season was going well at "Holly Gate Farm". The ewes gave birth within the warm and sheltered barn, carefully monitored by Peter. Jack came every day to clean and disinfect the areas. The relationship with Peter was back to normal, to the relief of both men. Susan came too, happy to spend time with Mattie and Ethan. The days could still be chilly, but the atmosphere in the kitchen was always warm and inviting.

In the lambing area, the ewes were comfortable in the extra straw bedding, with heat lamps on hand if needed. After every birth, ewes and lambs were put into a small pen or "jug", before being moved to the mixing pen with other ewes and lambs.

Dulap also came to offer his help. Peter felt less stressed with his arrival; his experience and confidence when dealing with the sheep were invaluable, especially if problems arose, as they inevitably did. Last year, a ewe was giving birth to a particularly large lamb; Dulap helped with the birth, and a visit from the vet was avoided. He gave each lamb a quick check, making sure it was breathing and suckling well. Peter and Jack dried them, applying an antiseptic solution to the navel. About half the ewes produced twins, and Mattie loved to help them adjust to their new world. She made sure they were feeding well on the colostrum-rich milk. Her special job was weighing the lambs and keeping careful records of the flock's progress. She had been re-assessing her role at the farm and had started to help Peter again. Everyone loved to see the fluffy, cuddly newborns.

Dulap went home each day. He had a feeling of unease and didn't want Imogen and Iris left too long. They had scheduled calls throughout the day. They hadn't heard from Samuel, but Imogen had talked to his sister a few times. She was told he was doing well, very much like his old self. 'Perhaps you would like to visit? Samuel was asking after you.' Imogen had firmly said 'no, there wasn't much point, as she had a new life now. She wished him well, but at the moment, coming to see him was out of the question.'

Mother and daughter were enjoying time in the garden. Imogen held Iris in her arms, showing her the early pots filled with yellow and purple crocus. The garden was a little overgrown, but she enjoyed weeding, making way for the roses she had ordered. Iris had proved to be a placid baby, looking at everything with interest.

A movement startled Imogen behind her. Turning around, Samuel faced her. She had never remembered his eyes being so blue, so piercing; it unnerved her. Holding Iris closely to her, she waited for him to speak.

'Good to see you, my dear. As you can see, I am well again and missing my wife. Oh...who is this? Your baby, Imogen?'

'Of course, Samuel. Mine and Dulap's; surely you remember my pregnancy? Why have you come all this way?'

'You won't come to me, so I thought I'd drive down. I'm not supposed to drive...still, I did all right. I want you to come back with me. Of course, we can no longer live at the vicarage...we'll find somewhere else. You can't bring your daughter, as she has nothing to do with me. Leave her here with that man. We'll live with my parents at first; they really won't mind, you know. In fact, they would be delighted.'

Imogen looked at Samuel in disbelief; he really must be mad. How could he think she would do anything of the sort? Trying not to panic, she answered, 'You have your own family now, Samuel. You will move on in time.'

'That's all very well, my dear, and they have been very good to me. However, you should have been there. You caused my illness in the first place because you left me. I seem to remember a promise at our wedding, to love, honour...in sickness and in health. When I was recovering, I thought of you as an angel; can you believe that? Still, it was that vision that kept me going; such a comfort, Imogen. Now, of course, I can see the truth. My wonderful angel was not the reality. Instead, it was my lovely wife who had abandoned me, living with an old man, and had given birth to his baby.' Samuel moved closer. His eyes were cold in their bright blue brilliance.

'Shall we go inside, my dear? It's cold, standing here, and I'd rather like a cup of tea.'

Imogen instinctively put her hand over Iris's head. Samuel noticed and clasped her arm. She cried out, 'You're hurting me; let go of my arm. We'll go inside then.' Brushing past him, she opened the door, removed the key, put it into her pocket and went into the kitchen. 'Sit down, Samuel, I'll put the kettle on. I won't be long.'

Imogen looked at the array of little pots on the windowsill: crocuses, blue and yellow iris and bell-like daffodils. She wondered how such joy-giving flowers could exist at the same time as having to deal with that madman in the next room. Then, she realised her phone was upstairs. How was she to get it and ring Dulap?

'Mister Dulap, mister Dulap!'

Sam Wood was making his way up to the farm, waving and calling. Not a young man, he was finding all this exertion difficult.

'Sam, what's up? Sit yourself down on one of these bales. You look all in.'

'Thankee, Mr Dulap. I hoped you'd be here. I was coming out of the house a short while ago, and a car passed me. It was that vicar bloke, I'm sure of it. He must be going to your cottage; I thought you'd like to know.'

'You're sure, Sam?'

'I sure as I can be. He didn't see me, but I saw him right enough.'

'I'm in your debt, Sam. I owe you a drink, my friend. Thanks.'

Iris had woken up, crying. Samuel called out, 'Give her to me, Imogen. You can't make tea with her strapped to you.'

'No, Samuel, no need for that...the water is in the cups...I'll just get the milk. Ready now...here you are.' Imogen sat Iris on her lap and grabbed a dummy, which the baby sucked on contentedly.

'Now, isn't this nice, my dear Imogen? I've travelled a long way to come here. We'll have our tea and be on our way home. The old man can look after your daughter. Pack little, only what's necessary.'

Imogen put down her cup and, scooping up Iris, ran up the stairs as fast as she could, locking the bathroom door against Samuel's banging and shouts.

'Go away, Samuel, leave us alone.'

'You are my wife, and you will do...'

Dulap ran into the cottage and up the stairs. 'Don't worry, Imogen, I'm here now...and as for you...' he manhandled Samuel down the stairs and out of the cottage. 'Never come here again, do you hear? If you do, I'll call the police. Do yourself a favour; go home and stay there. You have no business here!'

Imogen came down and locked the door. The safety of Dulap's arms was overwhelming. Now she and Iris were safe.

Dulap rang Peter to tell him what had happened. He wouldn't be in the next day, and after that Imogen would always come with him.

Samuel was angry by the turn of events, but he wasn't beaten; there had to be a way back. The strength of his adversary had surprised him, Dulap was a powerful man. A fight would have left him injured. His head hurt now. He'd better drive back...He wasn't supposed to drive at all.

That evening, after Dulap had bathed Iris and put her to bed, he sat with Imogen, enjoying a glass of wine and some peace. She was clearly shaken by what had happened.

'I should never have left you alone, my love. The safety of my family will be my priority from now on. I just didn't expect Samuel to do anything like this.'

Imogen curled into Dulap. 'We couldn't have known he would come here; it wasn't your fault. Honestly, I didn't recognise him as the same man I lived with. He could be cold and aloof at times, but there was a gentle side to him, too. He actually believed that I would leave Iris there and go away with him. I thought of running down the lane to get help, but I had Iris with me, and I wasn't sure I could run fast enough. When he suggested..no...ordered me inside, I went in quickly, getting the key. Otherwise, he might have locked me in, but he didn't seem to notice what I'd done. He wanted to hold Iris, but there was no way I was allowing that. I'll just refill my glass.' She continued, 'I couldn't message you because I'd left my phone in the bedroom, so I held Iris to me, shut my eyes, and prayed that you would come soon...and you did.'

Dulap stroked her hair. 'It's all right now, my love. You will never have to go through that again, I promise. As long as that's the end, and he doesn't bother you again, we'll leave it at that.'

'Do you think I should ring his sister? If his family doesn't know he came here today, then they should. Perhaps they could contact Mr Ruskin? I am sure he would need to know. As far as I'm aware, Samuel is still under his care.'

'Do you know them well?' Dulap asked.

'Yes, when we were first married, visits to his family were fairly frequent: Christmas, family occasions, things like that. I haven't got a big family; my father's dead, and Mum lives in Ireland. Maybe we could go for a visit? She would love to see us, and of course, she needs to see her granddaughter.'

'Of course, we can; I've never been to Ireland, and I'd like to meet her. As to contacting Samuel's family...let's leave it for the time being. Talk to Susan about it.'

Imogen's phone rang. 'Hello, is that Imogen? This is Marie, Samuel's sister.'

'Oh, do you know Samuel's been here? He'll be on his way back now. He must not come here again.'

'Oh, dear, I'm sorry, Imogen. Mum phoned me to say that Samuel had taken the car, and he's been gone since this morning. I said I would contact you in case you had seen him. None of us had any idea he was planning this. He has talked about you, of course, and said he wanted to save his marriage. It doesn't sound as though the meeting went well.'

'No, it didn't. I was on my own with my baby, Iris. He was aggressive and controlling towards me, and if Dulap hadn't come home, I don't know what would have happened.'

'I can only apologise, Imogen. We did not know...what can I say? Samuel has seemed so well lately.'

'We'll leave it at that then, shall we? As long as he stays away, I won't take further action, but if he comes here again, I will call the police. The marriage is over, and I've moved on. Talk to Samuel and make him understand.'

'We'll all try. He won't have access to a car in the future. I'll phone Mum back and tell her what happened. Bye, Imogen.'

It was decided that Samuel would go back and live with Marie and Dennis. Marie was concerned; if her brother's behaviour became extreme and he tried to see Imogen again, he might have to be hospitalised.

After a few weeks, all trace of his previous mental instability had gone, replaced by a happy, contented man who was getting ready for an early evening meal to celebrate Marie's birthday. She went to see how Samuel was getting on. He was not in his room or anywhere in the building. Even the shed and garage were searched.

'I'm taking the car to find him,' Marie said, trying to keep the panic out of her voice. 'He'll probably be on the shore.'

Samuel stood looking out at the green, white-flecked waves. How calm he was now...the madness of March, quite forgotten. He edged forward just a little...his shoes were getting wet...closing his eyes, he could hear someone calling him...not far out...his angel...

Marie ran along the beach as fast as she could. The pebbles slowed her down. Was he here? Yes, she saw him...going into the sea...

'Samuel! Samuel! Don't do this, come back, Samuel!'

Not struggling, just floating...until he went under.

Everyone was in shock at how this had happened. How could anyone have known what Samuel would do or stopped him? Marie blamed herself. 'I should have made sure he was not out by himself.'

'It's not your fault,' Dennis said, 'no one could have stopped him from going to see Imogen, and no one could have stopped his suicide. I'll let Mr Ruskin know, and I'd better ring Imogen. Your parents will arrive soon. We all feared for his state of mind. Even when we thought he was getting well, there was something terribly wrong.'

The inquest into Samuel's death recorded death by drowning because of a disturbed mind. Mr Ruskin gave medical evidence, and the family agreed to the verdict.

Imogen didn't attend the funeral but was upset by the death. She also felt a great relief, which was natural enough. They had been close once; she remembered him in her prayers.

CHAPTER THIRTY THREE

Dulap wanted to organise a trip with Ethan. So much had impeded their friendship, and although he had seen him many times at the farm, they needed a meaningful catch-up since Iris had been born. Before that was arranged, however, there was one visit he wanted to take, though he wasn't sure why. Leaving home before breakfast, he sauntered along the main road, past the local shop and the church, until he reached the turning into the woods where Ethan had gone the day Bates had died. Pausing briefly at the junction, Dulap continued along the narrow, overgrown path, stepping into the opening. Even on this cloudless day, all joyous feelings stopped here. He didn't go right to the edge of the pond. What was it about this place? It was as though the sun was forbidden to spread its rays across this still, stagnant water. Dulap wanted a complete closure of his battle with Bates; now he felt he finally would.

When he was a child, his father had told him that if a person took their own life or died accidentally, the spirit lived on in the place where they had died. True or not, Dulap felt a sense of Bates' presence. He felt no remorse; in fact, he was glad Bates was dead; to feel otherwise would be a lie. He would not come here again.

'Ethan,' Mattie called, 'Dulap's here.'

'Right, tell him I'm coming down.' He didn't know his friend was coming to see him, but he was certainly pleased. 'Hey, Dulap, great to see you. Can you stay for a while?'

'I can do better than that, lad. How do you fancy a trip to the moors? Bates may have gone, but we should see what's going on there. I wonder if Bates' sidekick has been promoted to Head gamekeeper?'

Ethan nodded. 'Just like old times, Dulap. I'm up for that.'

'Good, I've got plenty of tea and food in my rucksack.'

'How's Imogen, Dulap?' Mattie asked. 'You know, after what happened.'

'She's fine, really, and she would love to see you. Why not visit this afternoon?'

'I will, and have cuddles with Iris, too. See you both later.'

Dulap and Ethan walked out together, with the old ease in each other's company.

'How do you feel about walking here without seeing Bates?' Dulap asked.

'I feel good about it, I always felt nervous...you know...uneasy. I wonder who the head gamekeeper will be now. Could be Bates all over again.'

'That's true, lad, it could be. I must admit I'm tired of battling with people who kill birds and the absolutely pathetic laws we have in this country. These men should be jailed, and the owners fined heavily. They are doing better in Scotland, I believe.'

'Yes,' replied Ethan, 'they are tightening the laws there. These people need to be held accountable.'

The two had reached the woods, which bordered the moors, sitting down on old moss-covered logs, about to have something to eat. Dulap stood up suddenly. 'Stand here with me, lad. The moors look brilliant in the morning sun, don't they?' The purple heather had never looked so lovely to Dulap. He scanned the area with his binoculars but saw no one.

'You're right, Dulap. There seems to be a purple haze that covers everything, even the sky.'

'Before I saw you this morning,' Dulap answered, 'I went to Hadder's Pond.'

'Why? I can never go there again.'

'I know, lad, I know. There's no reason you should. It's a desolate place, right enough, but, in some strange way, I wanted to say "goodbye" to the man. I don't care that he's dead; we were enemies, and I would never have stopped opposing him, but I needed to see where he had died. Well, it's done now, and that's an end to it.'

Ethan remained silent, watching a pair of buzzards circling high above, calling. He was so engrossed in the moment that he didn't see someone walking towards them.

'We've been spotted, lad. Still, we're not actually on the moor, and I'm not moving. He doesn't look like a keeper. We'll stand our ground.'

'Hello, you must be Dulap and Ethan. Let me introduce myself. My name is Hugh Curtis, the Estate Manager. I'm not here to have a go. I like to walk about the estate sometimes, and I spotted you both. Actually, I'm glad to have met you. It's one of my jobs to appoint a new Head keeper, and my intention is to make the moors more wildlife-friendly. To be honest, the owners couldn't care less, as long as the money keeps rolling in via the shoot, but I am concerned about the birds that live and breed here. I warned Bates about his persecution of the harriers and other species, but he was a troublesome man; I was probably the only friend he had. His wife left him years ago, and he made enemies easily. Added to that, he had a terrible temper, and he drank too much. In the end, it was that combination, I am sure, that killed him.' Pausing, he added, 'Of course, Bates was afraid of you physically, Dulap, but it was more than that. He was afraid of who you are and what you stand for. He was jealous too; a lonely, bitter man, also aware I pitied him. Think about it for a moment. A lovely young woman moves in with you, and you become a father...well, you can imagine his reaction to that. And then, there was you, Ethan, a young man he spent years trying to catch. It was strange...the way he died, I mean. Still, I don't suppose I'll ever understand that. Anyway, I'm glad to have met you both.'

Dulap held out his hand, saying, 'I'm heartened by what you've said. I've seen you sometimes in "The Lapwing". If I see you there, I'll be glad to buy you a pint. Bye for now.'

They watched the retreating man. Ethan asked, 'Do you think he suspects about how Bates died?'

'No, lad, don't see how he can know. Still, he's a hard man to read. Likeable though, wouldn't you say?'

'Yes, I suppose so. Still, I don't trust him. Let's have something to eat, and I'm suddenly hungry.'

They sat on the log in silence until Dulap asked, 'made any plans, lad? You said something about a bird course.'

Ethan brightened. 'That's my news. I don't fancy university, that's for sure. All those years studying and then owing lots of money. No, I'm going to start a course at Birmingham; they meet every Saturday for six months. If I do well, it will give me a diploma, and then I can take it further if I want to. I'm also looking at volunteering at reserves; eventually, I may have to move away. What I'd really like to do is to be a warden on one of those remote islands, in Scotland, maybe. I enjoy being on my own. Jack said he would take me to Birmingham and bring me back.'

Dulap patted Ethan on the back. 'That's a good plan. I know it will lead to a wonderful future for you, you don't mind hard work. Tell you what, how about coming home with me? I know Imogen would love to see you, and Iris is crawling now.'

Ethan smiled. 'Yes, I'd like that, Dulap...hey, look at those buzzards up there. A pair, really high.'

Soaring, with raised wings, circling, wavering, the birds called noisily, with a constant, loud 'pee-yaeh', hovering in the still air with heavy wing beats. Eventually, they drifted away, and the two friends made their way back. The day had turned chilly; neither had a wish to stay on the moors today.

Imogen was surprised to see them back so early and was in high spirits. 'Hello, you two. I've had two visitors today, Mattie and Susan. We've been invited for Sunday lunch. A wonderful family get-together is just what I feel like. How are you, Ethan? Your Mum's been telling me all about your plans. Sounds good to me.'

Ethan still felt a little awkward around Imogen. He was attracted to her but tried not to show it. She had guessed but kept it to herself and didn't tell Dulap, always showing kindness towards the young man.

'Is Iris asleep?' Dulap asked. 'You like to see her, don't you?'

Ethan blushed slightly. 'I do, yes,' he answered. 'Could I...I mean.... could I stay the night? The sofa would be fine. It's just... I don't feel like going home yet, and I'd like to spend some time with Iris.'

'Of course, you can, Ethan. This is your second home. Stay whenever you like. In fact, stay tomorrow as well, and we can all go for Sunday lunch at Jack's together.'

'Thanks, Imogen.'

'That's settled then. Iris will be awake soon. She's really taken to you.'

Ethan was pleased. He was enchanted with the little girl, spending lots of time playing and reading to her. Tonight would be special, as Imogen had asked him to help bathe her and get her ready for bed.

Before that, Dulap looked after his daughter so that Imogen could show Ethan the garden, of which she was very proud.

'I like to plant wildflowers where I can. The Jacob's ladder is a recent addition, and I've just planted foxgloves over there in a shady spot. I sit here with Iris whenever I can. Look, there's a chiffchaff in that bush.' The small, greenish warbler hopped about with a constant bobbing of its tail.

'What else do you see in the garden, Imogen?'

'All the usual birds, blue tits, great tits, robins, blackbirds, but sometimes a visit from a pair of bullfinches, and at the moment a regular black-cap. Oh, I can hear Iris. Let's go in.'

For the first time in many months, Ethan felt pure contentment. After ringing Peter to tell him he was at Dulap's, he spent a happy hour with Iris, holding her in the air, which made her scream with excitement, and reading nursery rhymes to her.

As the nights could still be chilly, Dulap made a fire, and after supper, they settled down with some locally brewed beer. Imogen was still breastfeeding and was content with a cup of tea.

On Sunday morning, Ethan rose early, hearing baby cries. He could change and dress her. Then, he made a pot of tea while Imogen fed Iris.

'Did you know Dulap and I are going to Ireland to visit my Mum? My father died some years ago, and she remarried, then they moved over there. They grow all their own fruit and vegetables. Mum does most of it, and it's a full-time job. They buy eggs locally, which have been the same price for five years. Anything else can be bought in Castlerea, the nearest town to them. It's in Southern Ireland, in County Roscommon. We want to visit as often as we can. Next time we go, we would like you to come with us.'

'I'd like that. I've never been to Ireland. In fact, I've been nowhere much. Dad can't leave the farm, and now that Mum's living with Jack, they don't go away either. When I've finished my bird course, I'm going to volunteer to work on a reserve. A working holiday, you might say.'

Dulap joined them. 'Have you two had breakfast?'

'Just toast,' Imogen said, 'we'll be going to Jack's soon, so I'll make you a poached egg on toast. You can change Iris and put her clean clothes on. They're over there on the chair.'She was always amazed by how gentle and subtle Dulap's hands were, especially when he handled Iris, despite them being so large.

When they arrived at the farm, they found Jack and Susan preparing lunch. The kitchen was very warm; Susan needed a break.

'Sit down, Susan,' Jack said, 'I can do the rest. There's not much more to do. There's beer and soft drinks in the fridge, everyone, or spirits in the cupboard if you prefer. Peter and Mattie are on their way.'

'Let me look after Iris for a while. She's looking beautiful in her orange dress. Is that the one I bought for her?' Susan asked.

Imogen handed her daughter over, saying 'it is; it fits her perfectly. Ethan stayed with us on Friday and yesterday.' She sat back, feeling so relaxed, so happy. All the horrors of the past were slipping away from her; the terrible memories were part of another life.

Peter and Mattie came in. Susan was keen to catch up with her daughter, who had recently made some decisions about her future.

'I'm helping dad on the farm, part-time. Also, I'm going to convert two cow sheds into spaces where I can grow and then sell plants and flowers. Lots of people drive past the farm, and I'll put up signs at the end of the drive. It will take hard work, but it's a start.'

'Sounds like a plan, Mattie. I can help if you like. I've always got time on my hands.' Susan knew Mattie would never be content with a sideline of selling flowers. Maybe she would like to inherit the farm. Still, both her children were getting good, practical knowledge in their chosen careers.

Dulap stood behind Imogen. 'We have important news to tell you all; Imogen and I are getting married. It will be a simple affair at the registry office, with a reception at "The Lapwing". Where else? We'll wait until we come back from visiting Imogen's Mum in Ireland; we're planning to stay for three weeks. Ethan has kindly agreed to look after the cottage. He can stay there any time he likes.'

'That's all marvellous news,' said Peter. 'Let's all raise our glasses to Dulap and Imogen.'

CHAPTER THIRTY FOUR

At the beginning of July, Leona was told she had breast cancer. After the operation, a course of chemotherapy and radiotherapy would follow. She was stunned by the news but was unsure whether to tell Mona yet. She was coming at the weekend for a visit, with Mollie. Her plan was to wait until after the operation was over because they would fuss over her, and anyway, she would probably be completely cured of this disease.

'No Darnley?' Leona asked when they arrived.

'No,' answered Mona, 'He wanted to come, but he has so many work commitments at the moment. He sends his love and wants you to come and stay soon. Anyway, how are you?'

'Oh, I'm fine, my dear. It's a lovely day. I thought we might eat in the garden; the sandwiches are prepared. What would you both like to drink?'

'Tea, please. I'll come and help to bring everything outside,' Mollie chipped in.

Sitting round the garden table, in the sunshine, eating their lunch, the occasion seemed trouble-free. Leona decided today was not the right time to discuss her health problems.

'Your dahlias look good, Leona,' Mona said.

'Yes, they really are the mainstay of my summer pots. So many colours and types to choose from, although I prefer the smaller blooms to the more exotic varieties. Now, my dears, I want to hear all your news.'

Mollie looked at Mona and giggled. 'Mummy's expecting a baby in January. I couldn't wait to tell you. It's so exciting.'

'Oh, my goodness, what wonderful news; I'm so pleased.'

'We want you to be involved as much as possible, Leona. You will be one of the baby's grandmothers. I know you will love the baby, just as you do Mollie.'

Leona rose, saying, 'I'll make a fresh pot of tea. Back in a few minutes.'

Once in the kitchen, she shed a few tears. Such news, she wouldn't spoil it now.

To Mona's keen eye, she could tell her friend was visibly shaken. Was it just the news of the baby? Or something else? Looking at her closely, she knew Leona was not well. Something was not right. She would come back, on her own, and find out.

'Are you liking your school, Mollie?' Leona asked.

'Yes, I've made a friend called Dawn. I miss my friends at my old school, but Mummy says I can visit them in the holidays when I come to see you.'

'Is there anything I can do for you while I'm here?' Mona asked.

'No, my dear, everything is in order. You know how I like to keep busy. Just seeing you both is enough for me.'

'Well, I can do the washing-up at least. You'll not stop me from doing that.'

It was a beautiful afternoon. For a while, Leona could forget her troubles. Mona couldn't rid herself of her fears regarding Leona. She could see that the garden hadn't been weeded for quite a while. Before she went, she wiped the kitchen units, hung out the washing and washed the kitchen floor. Leona was usually fastidious about housework. Was she ill?

'Are you Busy, Darnley? I need a chat.'

Darnley's study was not big, but every bit of space was occupied, with an assortment of bookcases, filing cabinets and piles of files and papers. He kept it in a particular order, knowing how to find all the information he might need. An old, battered CD player was placed nearby on the large desk, which played his favourite jazz.

Holding out his hand to Mona, she sat next to him.

'Of course, my love, what's on your mind? Don't tell me you're fed up with me already?'

Mona laughed. 'You silly thing. As if? No, it's about Leona. I'm sure there's something wrong with her. I know her so well, and she wasn't her usual self.'

'Maybe she's coming down with a cold or something?'

Mona shook her head. 'No, it's more serious than that, and she's trying to keep it from me, so I'm going to find out what it is. I plan to turn up when she isn't expecting me. I can drop Mollie off at one of her friends on Friday, and I'll stay at Leona's overnight. Mollie's arranging a sleepover.'

'Sounds like a good plan. I hope it isn't anything serious. I'll make some time soon so that we can all go over together.'

Mona let herself into Leona's, expecting her to be busy somewhere in the house or garden. It had just gone ten, she called out. 'Leona, are you upstairs? I've come on a surprise visit.'

A bedroom door opened, and Leona came slowly down. 'Mona, I didn't expect you. Is there something wrong? I've overslept. Been a little tired lately. I'll make tea. Have you eaten?'

'Sit down, Leona. I'll do all that. Scrambled eggs are just the thing. When we've eaten, I want to talk to you.'

Leona protested, but Mona was having none of it. She ate very little, pushing the plate away.

'Come on, let's make ourselves comfortable in the sitting room. Take your tea with you,' Mona ordered. Leona was too exhausted to argue, deciding to be honest about the cancer. She was relieved to share her worries at last.

'I'm so glad you've come, my dear. I have breast cancer, a rather aggressive type. My operation is scheduled for next week; after that, a course of chemotherapy followed by radiotherapy.'

Mona held her friend's hands. 'I was right. I knew there was something wrong with you. You should have told me right away.'

'I know I should, I'm sorry. I didn't go to the doctor straight away because I didn't notice the signs. There was no lump, just a strange rash, and, at first, I thought little about it.'

'I see, when exactly do you have the operation?'

'Just a minute, I'll find the letter. Here we are, the operation is next Thursday. They say they will have to remove the breast completely, and lymph nodes too, to stop the cancer from spreading.'

'Now, listen to me, Leona, because this is going to happen. Tomorrow, I shall go home, tell Darnley and pack a few things I will need. I'll come back on Tuesday and stay to look after you after the operation. No...no buts. Then, we will take one day at a time. I'll do a shop as well, you have got little in. Oh, Leona, keep nothing from me again. Still, I know now. Can I see the letter?'

'Of course, here you are.'

'Right, it's very comprehensive. We'll know what to expect. A few days in hospital after the operation, with further visits to check on you. Then, a course of chemotherapy. Right, leave everything to me.' In the morning, Mona did a big shop, changed Leona's bedding and tidied around before leaving to collect Mollie.

'Right, Mollie, seat belt on. Good. I've had some bad news about Leona. She has breast cancer and goes into hospital next week for an operation. Now, I have an antenatal check on Monday, so I intend to come back on Tuesday and stay with Leona. She needs looking after.'

'Oh, Mummy, that's awful. Poor Leona. They will cure her, won't they?'

Mona sighed. 'I do hope so, darling. Chemotherapy isn't very nice, and she could be quite ill after that. I'll talk to Darnley and make sure he's working from home; he can do the school run. After it's all over, we'll have Leona over here for a complete rest.'

'That will be nice, Mum. I really miss her.'

Darnley was there to meet them. 'My two favourite girls. How was the trip?'

Mollie rushed to give him a hug. 'Leona's not well and has to have an operation.'

'That's bad news.' He turned to Mona. 'I know it's early in the day, but I think you need a gin and tonic. You look washed out.' Later on, when Mollie was in bed, the couple talked about the situation.

'I was right, Darnley; Leona is very ill. If she'd told me earlier, I would have taken her to see a doctor right away. I could see that things had been neglected. The grass hadn't been mowed for weeks. Pots of tulips, long past flowering, needed lifting, and the house... well, not like Leona to neglect things. Her operation is on Thursday, so I thought I would go back on Tuesday and get everything sorted out for when she comes out of the hospital. Of course, I will keep all my appointments regarding the baby.'

'I see. Well, there's no reason to worry about Mollie. She and I will look after each other. I'll spend the foreseeable future working from home.'

'That's great, Darnley. It's just a case of juggling everything. I'll need to come home for my scan, but don't worry, I'll look after myself too.' She put her arms around the big man, continuing, 'It might be a difficult time for all of us, but with you to love and support me, I'm so hopeful about the future.'

The operation went well. Leona returned home, feeling relieved it was over. Mona had cleaned the house, making everything ready for her friend's return. She was a perfect patient. There followed three weeks of healing and sharing time with Mona. Darnley and Mollie came and stayed a few days; it all seemed to go well. At twelve weeks, Mona had the scan, which was exciting for them all. Leona was amazed to see the baby forming; she had never seen a scan before.

'Oh, look at that. I can see the head and little limbs.' Then she said, 'don't you think you should go home now, my dear? I am feeling much better, and you need to look after yourself. I'm starting chemotherapy soon, but I'll get through that. You need to be with your family now.'

Mona was doubtful. 'I've read that the aftereffects of the treatment can be awful, and what about the injections you have to give yourself? I know you're dreading having to do that, so if I stay for longer, I can do the injections for you.'

During this time, Malcolm visited regularly, coming every week to see how Leona was getting on. Mona was pleased to see him, too. His new relationship was going well, but above all else, he wanted to be a proper part of Mollie's life. They agreed regular meetings should be set up, with Mollie staying with him every other weekend. For now, though, Leona's recovery was a priority. When Mona had to return home, he drove Leona to the hospital for her appointments. Over this difficult time, Malcolm became indispensable. A deep friendship formed between them; he looked after her with care and affection. When Leona began to lose her hair, Malcolm shaved her head, replacing it with a scarf. Leona didn't wear it but wore a wig if she went out.

Leona seemed to recover well; the doctors were pleased with her progress. Everyone looked forward to the birth of the baby. The future looked hopeful.

CHAPTER THIRTY FIVE

Peter stood, drinking his morning coffee, his back against the lambing barn, now empty, swept and cleaned. From the start, he had been determined to do everything right. He never cut corners; his education in animal husbandry was self-taught, backed up with the experience of Dulap and Jack, who had been indispensable. Against all the odds, he had made a success of farming. But to what end? From the start, he had wanted it to be a family business. Susan told him she would stay as long as he made it work. He had, but she had still left him to be with the man who had given him so much help.

Mattie had always stood by him, but he doubted her idea of growing and selling flowers would amount to too much. Ethan had no interest in the farm, being out most of the time, or studying in his bedroom.

He suddenly shivered in the morning breeze, feeling hot. His body ached; it felt like his previous illness, which had sent him to bed for the best part of a week. Work had been impossible. Jack proved to be a genuine friend, helping Mattie to keep things going.

Dulap was still in Ireland with Imogen and Iris. They had stayed on for another two weeks. The sheep needed to be dipped in the plunge pool, and the lamb sales were coming up; a few old ewes were to be sold, too. With tupping time near, two rams were to be bought. So, if he were ill, Dulap would not be on hand to help.

Mattie came out, still in pyjamas and a dressing gown. 'Morning, Dad, you look worried. Is everything o.k.? Do you want breakfast?'

'Not much for me, Mattie. Fresh coffee would be good, though. Have we got a couple of paracetamol?'

'Yes, I think so. Are you feeling unwell?'

'A little, it will pass, I'm sure. Now, I need to talk to you. The ewes need to be moved onto the fresh pasture and given supplements, so they will put on weight, ready for the rams.'

'Are you buying rams?'

'Yes, two should be enough to do the job. Do you want to come with me to the market?'

'Sure, Dad, when are you going?'

'Thursday. I'll give Jack a ring to see if he's free to come too.'

During the next few days, Peter felt worse. With Mattie's help, they moved the ewes onto suitable pasture after selecting the ones he would sell from his flocks of North of England Mule cross-bred sheep with the typical black and white faces. The trip to the market went well, returning with a pair of good rams and several mule lambs.

Two days later, Peter collapsed and was ordered to bed by Mollie. Jack and Susan came to assess the situation, with Susan immediately taking charge.

'I'm going to move in until you're better, Peter. No buts. We've been here before, remember, and you were very ill. I find this worrying, though, and wonder whether this life you've chosen is right for you. Are you really suited to this outdoor life, Peter? Anyway, we won't discuss this now. When are Dulap and Imogen due back?'

'Not sure, maybe a week longer? Something like that.'

'I'll ring Dulap and explain the situation. For the time being, Jack will help Mattie. Try to sleep now, Peter.'

'I will, thanks Susan. Maybe we should leave Dulap alone for now. I don't feel right about them coming back earlier on my account.'

'If Jack and Mattie can manage for now, that's fine, but no one deal with sheep-like Dulap. We'll see how it goes.'

Susan went downstairs. She was going to ring, anyway. Jack would need to get back to his own farm, and she couldn't handle a pair of rams with Mattie.

'How's Peter?' Jack asked.

'He'll sleep now. He should have been in bed days ago. I want to call for a doctor, but he doesn't want me to. I've made a bed up in the spare room for myself. Where's Mattie?'

'She said she had some accounts to finish. I know she's really worried about Peter and the farm. She's not saying much.'

'I see. I'll find her soon. Want a coffee?'

'Yes, please. Shall I ring Dulap?'

'Definitely, Jack. We really need him here. He'll understand. I've also had an idea, but I need to run it past Mattie and Peter. I'll tell you about it later.'

Mattie was sifting through bills and receipts in the farm office when Susan walked in.

'Hello Mum, how's Dad?'

'I've put him to bed; he's asleep now, hopefully until morning. It's a repetition of before, so I'm staying until he's better.'

'Oh good. I'm glad you'll be around. I miss you.'

Susan gave Mattie a hug. 'I miss you too, darling. Jack will have to go back, and he's got his own work to do. He's going to ring Dulap and explain the situation, asking him to come back early. Imogen will understand. Somehow, when Dulap's around, everything seems better, don't you find that?'

Mattie nodded. 'I do; he's such a kind man and a remarkable person as well. I think of him as a second father. Does that sound silly?'

'Not at all. By the way, talking about Dulap, I wondered if he had anything to do with helping Ethan when he was caught by Bates?'

'I don't know, but whoever it was, we should be grateful to him.'

'I agree,' said Susan. 'There's something else I want to talk to you about: the future of the farm. I know you do a lot to help but unless you are truly committed to the business, Peter will find it increasingly hard to manage, especially where his health is concerned. Do you agree?'

'I suppose I do, Mum. To be honest, I just don't know if I can make that kind of promise right now. I'm uncertain about things. I'm sorry.'

'Don't be, Mattie. This might solve the problem.'

Jack joined them. 'I've been talking to Dulap. They will be back the day after tomorrow. Both are concerned about Peter and want to help. Sounds like they have had a great time over there.'

'That's wonderful news, isn't it, Mum?'

'It is. Now, while I have you both here, I want to tell you about my idea. I'm not sure how this all works, or even if it's possible, but maybe we could find an apprentice who is interested in farming and would work here for a wage, of course. Are there such schemes, Jack?'

'It might be possible; someone within the local community. Leave it with me, and I'll make some enquiries.'

'Of course,' continued Susan, 'I'd need to discuss it with Peter. He may not like the idea.'

Peter slept until late in the morning. His temperature had gone down slightly, but Susan wasn't taking any chances and ordered him to stay in bed. She sat him up to drink his tea and eat a little scrambled egg.

'How do you feel today, Peter?'

'About the same. Sorry, I can't eat the egg. I feel less tired, but my body aches. Don't worry, I'll stay in bed. Is Jack still here?'

'He is, but he'll have to go back later. However, Dulap and Imogen are on their way back, so you needn't worry about those sheep of yours.' She paused, then said, ' How would you feel about getting a young person to help you with the daily running of the farm? A sort of...apprenticeship.'

'Is that really necessary? The farm's in good shape, and I'll soon be back on my feet. Mattie's here and Dulap is always on hand to help.'

Susan shook her head. 'Yes, but Mattie only works part-time, and her future is uncertain. Ethan has no interest in the farm, Jack has his own farm to run, and Dulap is no longer a young man. Besides, he has a new life now with a wife and child. Is it fair to always rely on him? This is the second time you have been ill and unable to work. You must face facts, Peter.'

Peter sighed and fell back on his pillows. 'You can look into it if you like, but I make no promises. Thanks for being here for me, Susan.'

Susan took his hand and kissed it. 'I'll get a bowl of warm water and give your face and hands a wash. Maybe you can have a bath tomorrow. Can I get you anything else?'

'Just a glass of water, please and my farming magazines. They're on the kitchen sideboard.'

Dulap breezed into Peter's bedroom, who was sitting up in bed, reading. Peter thought how fit and healthy his friend looked, even though he was fifteen years his senior. A man born to be loved, perfectly at home on the land. How glad he was to see him.

'How are you, Peter? The old illness getting you down? Tell me what needs to be done.'

'Great to see you, Dulap. I'm sorry you had to cut your holiday short. Mattie knows what's being done. She'll fill you in. The ewes have been moved to pasture, ready for the rams. I bought two.'

'Excellent. Is Ethan around?'

'No, he's been at your cottage since you left. Mattie's doing the paperwork in the farm office. I'm hoping to come downstairs tomorrow if Susan allows it.'

Dulap laughed. 'Like that, is it? She's a good woman.'

'Yes, she is. I miss her. To be honest, I'm rather lonely. I'd like a companion. Still, time for that.'

Susan came in. 'Meal in ten minutes. The patient can eat downstairs if he feels up to it.'

Peter grinned, 'try to stop me. I'm feeling much better already, and my appetite is coming back. No more bedrest.'

'I agree,' Susan replied, 'but that doesn't mean back to the farm. You still have to take things easy. Agreed?'

'Agreed.'

Mattie came in. 'I've finished the accounts, Dad. I need you to check them.'

'I'll do that tomorrow. There's some ordering to be done as well.'

Jack came back for the meal. It was a pleasant evening. Peter enjoyed the company; it was like old times, but not quite. Nothing would ever be the same again.

The next day, Susan went home, having made Mattie promise to ring if Peter felt worse. He was not to step out of the house at all, not even into the yard, until he was completely recovered.

Ethan had enjoyed his stay at the cottage, keeping everything clean and tidy, just as he did in his own room at the farm. He could stay one more night, catching up with Imogen's news about the holiday. The break had clearly been of significant benefit to her, spending time with her mother and rekindling their relationship; it had meant so much to mother and daughter. They would go back next year and Ethan was invited too.

In an all too rare conversation with Peter, Ethan explained his plans to him.

'I've been working hard to get an excellent result on my course. That will finish next summer, and I've been looking at various options to further my career. I will always want to come back here but my plan is to work abroad for a year. There's a scheme in India to breed vultures and return them to the wild. Of course, it's voluntary with board and lodging, but I'd really like to go. What do you think?'

'I think,' replied Peter, 'that's a wonderful opportunity. You go, Ethan. I'll take care of your expenses and you'll need some spending money. I'd like to look at the details with you.'

'Thanks, dad, the application needs to be in soon. I feel so excited about it.'

'Have you told your Mum yet?'

'No, but I'll see her tomorrow. You know, Dad, I'm sorry I never took much interest in the farm. I just couldn't whip up the enthusiasm, I suppose.'

'None of that matters now, Ethan. I want you to do whatever makes you happy. You go, with my blessing.'

CHAPTER THIRTY SIX

Leona was getting to the end of her treatments. She had frequent visits from Mona, and also Malcolm, who had been with her in her darkest moments. He was a happier man since meeting Anna and talked to Leona about it.

'Our long-term aim is to live together, maybe get married, but for now, we have agreed to stay in our own places, seeing each other as much as possible. I have Mollie to consider as well. I want her to have my full attention when she comes to stay. She's very excited about the upcoming birth.'

'Oh, yes, she is, and I'm going to be an honorary grandmother. Mona's having a boy, and I've been trying to knit something for him, but my skills are a bit rusty.'

'Well, I'll give the knitting a full inspection when it's finished. You must be so relieved to be coming to the end of your hospital visits.'

'There won't be an end to those, I'm afraid; six monthly check-ups and other treatments for some time. Just as long as the cancer doesn't come back.'

'I see. Well, I'm at your disposal for all those trips.'

'Thank you, Malcolm. I'm so grateful to you. Now, I hope you'll stay for lunch. Just a simple quiche and salad, with tomatoes and cucumber from my greenhouse.'

'I'm impressed, Leona, it's good to see you getting on with our life. Do you feel better in yourself?'

'I do. I'm going to see my little family in Lincolnshire next week. Darnley will collect me and bring me back; Mona's getting too big to get behind the wheel. I'm looking forward to the change. They do spoil me so much. Darnley rarely works on a Friday, so I go then. He's such a kind man; he always makes me smile.'

'Well, give them my best when you see them.'

Darnley came to collect Leona early, only by half an hour, but even if he'd come much earlier, Leona would have been ready. She had been up since five, taking a leisurely bath, then breakfast and doing minor household tasks before her departure. Her case had been packed the day before. She was looking forward to her time away, and they always tried to persuade her to stay longer. She wanted to, but this time she had yet another hospital appointment to assess her progress. Still, she was over the worst and a week away with her lovely family was all she needed right now.

'Right, Leona, let's get you home. Everything's prepared for your visit. I think you will like your bedroom; bright and colourful. Got its own on-suite, too. There's tea and coffee-making facilities, even a small fridge. We want you to feel just like you would in your own home. You are part of the family now.'

'That all sounds wonderful, Darnley. All the previous months of operations and awful treatments are just fading away. A bright future starts now.'

'Good, good, absolutely capital, Leona. We have a few trips planned for you, but only if you want to. This is your holiday.'

'I'd like a trip to Louth. What's it like?'

'Very nice. It's kept its old-fashioned feel if you know what I mean. A much sought-after place to live, but the houses are very expensive. We can certainly have a day there. Do you like cheese, because there's quite a famous cheese shop?'

'Yes, I'll take some back with me. You must be excited about becoming a father. Won't be long now.'

'I am indeed. I never thought it would happen to me or meet someone like Mona and the lovely Mollie. Having the time of my life and loving every minute.'

'Thought of any names for the baby yet?'

'Didn't think it would be so difficult to come to an agreement about a name. Mona and I have rather different choices. She rather likes biblical names, whereas I like unusual English ones that used to be popular but have fallen out of favour. Lionel, for instance.'

'You'll both think of one to suit when the time comes.'

'Now, changing the subject, Leona, how are you doing now, after your operation? Mona is concerned that you might keep things from her again.'

'No, I made a promise that I will keep her informed about everything, good or bad. I feel fine, I really do. I want to be given the all-clear. It may come back, but regular checks will spot that. It takes five years after the surgery to be really sure.'

Mona came out to greet them, looking very pregnant and happy.

'Leona, give me a hug. So pleased you're here; you look well. Mollie's at school, and Darnley will fetch her later. She's dying to see you. Come on, I want to show you your bedroom.'

'What an enchanting room,' Leona said, 'It's like something from a bygone age.'

'Yes, that's exactly what it is. Darnley kept this room just as it was. The wallpaper dates back to the Edwardian era. The fireplace is intact; in fact, it's been swept recently. Darnley will light it for you later.'

'Well, if it's not too much trouble, I would like that. I can see there are no radiators.'

'I'll get Darnley to bring your case up. I have a few things to talk to him about, so come down when you're ready. Help yourself to anything you want.'

Left alone, Leona looked around the room. The bed was a four-poster, with pale yellow velvet curtains; the lead paned windows had matching curtains. In one corner stood a small, white dressing table with a floral-patterned padded chair. A wardrobe and chest of drawers lined one wall, while the bedside table held a crystal vase filled with cream and pink roses. The cream carpet matched the wallpaper, while two fluffy rugs lay on either side of the bed.

Leona always abandoned her footwear in the hall, so she opened her case to retrieve her slippers. Climbing onto the bed, she ran her hand over the silken bedspread, then lay down for a few minutes.

Mona wanted to get Darnley's opinion about Leona. 'How does she seem to you?'

'Well, you can see for yourself, my love. Considering all she's been through, I would say she's bearing up well. Now, I want you to relax and stop worrying. I've prepared the vegetables for later. Let's have a cup of tea and my homemade scones. I've got the best china out. See if Leona's ready to come down.'

'I'm so glad you like the room,' Darnley said, 'when I looked around the house, with a view of buying it, I kept the bedroom just as it is. It is beautiful.' He looked at his watch. 'Oh, time to fetch Mollie, I'd better go.'

Fifteen minutes later, Mollie rushed into the sitting room.

'I'm so glad you're here, Leona. What do you think of the flowery bedroom?'

'I love it, Mollie. In fact, it's enchanting and most unusual. I tried the bed for a while when I came. Never slept in a four-poster before. Tonight, I shall pull the curtains all the way around so that I can be really cosy. Then, in the morning, draw them back to look at the pretty room.'

Mollie laughed. 'Yes, you can do that. I like the two pictures of cats. Have you seen them?'

'I have, they are nice. In fact, there are a lot of pictures, which I shall study carefully.'

The visit to Louth on Sunday and a walk in the Wolds were enough for Leona; she enjoyed both, buying her rather expensive cheeses to take back. The rest of her stay was spent in and around the house, insisting she made some meals and enjoying using all the modern gadgetry, including a bread maker and a dishwasher, which were new to her.

It was with regret that she had to leave the following Friday. Mollie was going too, to spend the weekend with Malcolm. Leona was to join them at Christmas and then stay for the birth.

On Saturday, Leona spent the afternoon at Malcolm's and talked about her visit.

'They do have a lovely house, and they are happy for me to help with the garden. Darnley's going to make an order for the spring. It's too late to plant tulips, but I'll do my best. I had a wonderful time. They still haven't decided on a name for the baby, though. They will, by the time he's born.'

Towards the middle of December, Leona went for a check-up. There was a problem; another operation may be necessary. The cancer had spread, and the diagnosis was not good. Leona was devastated and wondered whether to ring Mona. She decided against it.

That night she lay in her bed, tired but unable to sleep. The room was dark, but she was warm enough. Clasping her hands together, Leona prayed. Repeating her words, she prayed for a recovery. Not aware of how long she lay there and prayed, she was suddenly aware of a presence beside her bed. A great calm took hold of her, surrounding her, wrapping her body into a deep, untroubled sleep. In the morning, the feeling remained for some time and a joy she could not describe. Then Leona knew, without a doubt, the cancer was gone.

She waited a day, gathering her thoughts, then phoned Mona.

'Leona, you sound strange. Is everything alright with you?'

Leona took a deep breath, then said, 'Yes, my dear, something wonderful has happened to me. I can't put it into words really...the cancer has gone...it's gone.'

'Who was that on the phone?' Darnley asked.

'Leona, telling me the cancer has gone. I mean...we know that so why did she phone to tell me? She sounded a little odd. I expect she'll explain when she sees me. What do you make of it?'

Darnley leaned back on his chair. 'Maybe it's the realisation and the relief that's overtaken her. She wanted to share her happiness with you. Nothing to worry about, I'm sure.'

'Yes, I'm sure that's it. What else could it be? By the way, I've been thinking. What do you think about Leona moving here permanently? She could sell her house and really be part of the family, especially with the baby coming. Would you be agreeable?'

'I'm happy with that if you are. I've grown very fond of Leona myself, and it makes sense. We'll mention it at Christmas.'

CHAPTER THIRTY SEVEN

Leona's consultant confirmed what she already knew: there was no sign of cancer anywhere in her body. She was at a loss to explain it, and Leona was not about to enlighten him. She was to come back in six months for a check-up.

Now, free of the disease, at last, Leona busied herself with plans for Christmas. She spent Christmas Eve with Malcolm and Anna, and then Darnley collected her early Christmas morning.

During her stay, Mona talked to her about the future. 'Darnley and I would love you to move here. You could always go back home at any time if you wished. What do you think?'

'I think you are such wonderful friends, and sometime soon, I will certainly sell my house and come and live here. It will be the natural thing to do. Just give me another year to spend time in my dear house and garden. You understand, my dear?'

Mona hugged her. 'Of course I do, whenever you're ready. The flowered bedroom is reserved just for you. Now that's settled, I want to ask you something.'

'I think I know what it's about: the phone call to you before Christmas. You must promise not to tell anyone, not even Darnley.'

'I promise.'

'So,' continued Leona, 'do you believe in miracles? Because that's the only way I can explain what happened to me.'

'Oh, my goodness. I'm not sure. Tell me.'

Leona recounted her experience of that night in as much detail as she could remember. 'It was such a profound, spiritual encounter. His presence, and the overwhelming feeling of peace afterwards; it felt as though I was being wrapped around in a comfortable, protective shield. I actually felt the cancer retreating from my body. I didn't need to have it confirmed by my doctor, but when I went to my hospital appointment, the consultant was at a loss for words.'

Mona looked at Leona for a while; she could see the effects of the visitation, even now. Taking her hands, she said, 'I absolutely believe you. Now, come and look at the baby's room. Everything's ready for him.'

'The nursery looks lovely, Mona.'

'Darnley did it all, you know, even the painting and the murals on the walls; we liked the aquatic theme. The baby won't be sleeping in there at first, of course, but I can feed him in the rocking chair.'

'Any agreement on the name yet?'

'We both like Lawrence, so it's Lawrence Barnaby.'

Dulap was bouncing Iris on his knee. 'You like that, don't you? My arms are getting heavy, so I'll put you down for a crawl.'

'Peter decided not to find someone to help around the farm then?' Imogen asked.

'That's right, I don't blame him. He can manage on his own with Mattie's help for the time being, but he'll have to take care of his health to avoid periods of illness. I'm sure he'll be fine.'

'Mattie's happy about that, is she?'

'Seems so. She's dropped the flower idea; maybe the farming life suits her best, after all. There's talk about her going to agricultural college.'

'Good. Ethan still set on his wildlife adventure?'

'Very much so. Will do the lad a world of good. I like to think that my encouragement has been beneficial.'

'Of course, it has, Dulap. All those years of friendship, sharing your knowledge with him, not forgetting trips to the woods and the moors. I don't know what the two of you got up to, legal or otherwise. Still, I know better than to ask.'

Dulap laughed. 'It was the two of us fighting the common enemy.'

'Would you like to see the end of the annual shoot?'

'Yes, the whole thing is a sham, and wherever it takes place, wild birds are shot, poisoned or caught in crow traps. There will always be bad gamekeepers and landowners who don't care. Much better if the moors were managed for the preservation of wildlife. By the way, I promised to see Jack. Anything you need from the village shop?'

'I'll check and make a list. By the way, I went for a walk yesterday to the church; good that it's always open during the day. I didn't see anyone else, so I sat for a while and lit a candle for Samuel. His life was so tragic. After that, I did something I hadn't been able to do for a while; I stood opposite the vicarage...it felt strange and sad. I had to do it, though. Lay the ghosts, perhaps. Anyway, Susan's coming over soon. Are you going to see Jack about anything in particular?'

'No, not especially. Haven't seen him for a while, that's all.'

'See you later then. Here's the list. No urgency for it.'

Susan came. 'Dulap arrived, the two of them clearly had an agenda, They were up to something. Jack couldn't wait for me to go.'

'Oh, really. Dulap said nothing to me, but, come to think of it, he seemed cagey. Iris has got one of those baby colds. She's asleep, so sit down; I'll make some coffee. I'm glad Peter's better.'

'Yes, fully recovered and back to work with a vengeance. I've never seen him enjoying his work so much. So good to see.'

'It is. What about Mattie?'

'She's happy working with him for the time being but needs to find some friends. Peter's going to pay for driving lessons, then she can get out, maybe join a group. Ethan's off on his working holiday soon. I worry about him, of course, like I did with all that business with Bates. I never did quite understand all that.'

Dulap walked to the shops and then made his way to Jack's farm. The kitchen table was littered with farming magazines; Jack was flicking through them. 'I never seem to have time to read these. Don't know why I keep getting them? Still, some articles have proved useful. How are you, Dulap? Glad to see you. I've got everything bagged up. It's all in two black bin liners.'

'Good man, I'll take them away. I know what to do with them. You can go back to being just a regular farmer, and I'm the odd-job man. You took an enormous risk, though, Jack. Being seen in and around the moors put me in the frame for a while, but there was never enough proof on either of us. That day, when Bates attacked Ethan, I was really worried, I can tell you. I tried to stop the lad from going there on his own because I knew one day, Bates would catch him. The worst of it was that I wasn't there to help him. You were brilliant though, Jack, all dressed in black.'

'I really thought we would fight Bates forever. I was stunned when I heard of his death.'

'The man was a menace,' replied Dulap, 'but even he didn't deserve a death like that. Ever been to Hedder's Pond?'

'Once, years ago, I was going to look at the place just because it had such a terrible reputation, but I never did. Bates was drunk, and the drowning was just an unfortunate accident. Was there anything more to it?'

'That's about it,' replied Dulap. 'Now, let's have the bags. You don't want Susan finding them.'

Towards evening, Dulap wandered to the moors before returning home. They had lost much of their colour during the winter. Dark skies were forming, full of dark grey clouds. To the right of his gaze, the heavens were a vivid red. The moors were silent now. He made a wish that the harriers would return next year, nest and raise their chicks without persecution. He would be forever vigilant, watching silently.

THE END